CARDS AND CLAY

Cards and Clay

---

one man two worlds

IAN COCHRANE

Ingramspark

Cover design: Marcelo Figueredo
Cover image: `Il Traditore' by Fabiana Belmonte

"Only mystery allows us to live, only mystery"
... Federico García Lorca

For John. Still looking for a little black cloud in a dress
... IC, Melbourne, Australia, 2019

CONTENTS

X - CONTENTS

XII - CONTENTS

XIV - CONTENTS

ABOUT THIS BOOK AND AUTHOR

The story of known unknowns, a search for answers, the inconvenience of unreasonable coincidence, and a timeless residue that can linger after tragic events.

Wanderlust has lured the author to The Americas, Europe, Asia and the South Pacific, with work taking him to India, Africa, Korea, and the highlands of Papua New Guinea.

He has penned several books including –

- Indian Summers – Mumbai and Beyond – Warm recollections of an Indian sojourn
- Everything Under the Sun – Australian Short Stories of Light and Shade from A to Z
- A World Away – Global Short Stories of Light and Shade from A to Z

His Australian Outback short story `A Splendid Memory' was included among the 2013 non-fiction Cowley Literary Award finalists. There have also been several travel and food features published in The Australian.

iancochrane.com.au

| 1 |

The year is 2019, and the cards are on the table, pulled from a lightly embossed case of finely pressed metal. Michael squints; twenty-one cards in all, washed-out and faded reds to browns, the backs floral with a diamond cobble pattern. The childlike pictures are cryptic, with human figures in Medieval garb. There are no suits, names, or titles. There are no numbers.

For a moment, he is distracted, nods to a dog walker and listens to the clamour and clang of a Melbourne morning tram. Hints of fruit toast and coffee hang on the early autumn air. He gazes inside the open double door, Maria's cafe cosy and quiet, with bentwood chairs and more round tables. The wooden bench groans under the weight of a silver coffee machine, the top of Maria's head a black bob, these days bewitched with a streak of white. She spies Michael and steps to the side, hand on her hip. She strokes her hair. Oversized reading glasses are scarlet, and her lipstick is the same.

She shouts out. "Sooo predictable, Lover, so serious, the squinting when you worry. *Si*, always the books, the study, and newspapers."

1

He shrugs and returns to his cards. Maria is captivated, and she mumbles to herself. "*Si*, the curls are finally gone grey. But the same blue jeans and pretty shirt as always, the vest of corduroy, the college look for the middle age gentleman." Maria has been here from the very start, these days helping out an only son, but her cooking and coffee are still sublime.

She is suddenly gone from her coffee machine and stands by Michael. He looks up and wonders where the years have gone. Her pursed lips are older, with smile lines in each corner. She puffs on her cigarette and wipes the other hand on her apron, a picture of the *Castel dell'Ovo* with the word '*Napoli*' emblazoned across her belly. She is curious. "Lover, it is Friday, even for you sooo early. This is not good, and I worry. You let Maria's special coffee go cold. And look at you, your paper all folded and these cards." Her eyes narrow. "I am thinking you have something to tell your Maria?"

Michael stares into her eyes and explains the cards were left behind by Don, a young writer friend from years ago, and the cards were a gift from his French mother on his sixteenth birthday. Don was killed in 1997, in his late twenties, but now back to haunt Michael. He shuffles in his seat, uncomfortable with the thought of Don's cards relegated to the back of a sock drawer after the funeral.

Maria remembers the accident and falls silent, eyes wide, her hands still. "Ah, *si* Lover, sooo shocking, and terrible for you. *Si,* I remember, me young and new back then." One hand settles on Michael's shoulder, Maria's eyes first drawn to the metal card case. "Mmmm. *Bellissimo.*"

Michael detects a change in Maria's manner, an obvious frown and her dark eyes jumping to the cards themselves. "So Lover, you have these all this time and are not showing your Maria."

But for Michael, it is no longer just about the cards, not after a phone call from Don's best friend two days ago. Michael has not seen Robbo since the funeral. Robbo is downsizing, and his wife has demanded Don's boxes must go, after being stored amongst a lifetime of clutter and stuffed in a corner of the family garage for twenty-two years. According to Robbo, the boxes of notes are a rambling diary of sorts, Don's innermost thoughts that no one else could bear to read after the young writer was killed. Robbo has sent all the boxes to Michael - a historian - with no mention of Don's sister.

Michael runs a finger along the smooth edge of one dog-eared card apart from the others: a skeleton on a horse with a long-handled scythe. Frightened folk kneel on the ground among bodies in bits and pieces.

Maria leans even closer, head cocked to one side, eyelashes impossibly long, and her perfume sweet like syrup. For a moment, Michael is terrified at the thought of an imminent bear hug but instead gets a gentle shoulder rub. She sucks on her cigarette, gathers up the cards from the table, flips each on its back and counts them as she goes. Her lips form a perfect circle. "Ooh," she croaks, "these cards, Lover, so very old." Silence again. Maria finally stops counting, her eyes on the single card still in Michael's hand. "Mmmm, I am thinking a type of Tarot of course, only different." She frowns again. "And *si*, there is a change coming for you in these cards Lover. I see it, something here that will soon come to an end."

His trance is broken. "Maria, you've seen these before?" She shakes her head and drops the cards back on the table. "No, no, not the same, Lover. But like them, *si*, me just a pretty young girl." There is a wry smile. "My grandmother's family, *Italiano*, but funny people up north, the winters long, the snow and mountains." She nods. "They are readers of cards in the old days. Cards like yours, Lover."

Michael flips his skeleton card over, picture down, and remembers his mother's card nights, the fortnightly games held in the kitchen due to the dining table cluttered with his builder father's books. Michael was never one for card games but remembers a two-pack Uruguayan concoction called 'canasta.' He preferred to play football with the Aboriginal kids from the mission ruins near the family home. But these cards have the same flowery back as his mother's.

He squints and flips another card on its back, all bent and worn, others with missing corners. Maria pouts and screws up her eyes. "So, I am thinking of your cards, *si*, a Tarot. Mmmm. But Lover, there is one card that is missing." She nods. "*Il Traditore*. You call him 'The Traitor.'"

Michael grimaces and pokes the cards back in their case then rises to his feet but forgets to pay for his coffee. Maria is left bemused, hands now on both hips, cigarette tucked in the corner of her mouth.

The office is just minutes away, and he drifts in the general direction. Street trees cast early shadows on steel tram tracks that shimmer and sparkle. Suddenly, he is on the footpath outside the office and gazes across the road, a line of cars to the University entrance. He turns and checks his vest pocket, Don's cards are still there. The other hand is on a fence post, cold cast iron, the black paint flaky, the pickets bolstered by thin brick piers. The gate squeaks, heavy on its hinges.

The building is one part of a Victorian terrace, inherited by Michael's old boss Clive, from a French Teacher aunt. A monstera plant crowds the front courtyard, the leaves dark green and dusty. Michael is startled by a screech from the tram terminus. He brushes cobwebs from his Paisley shirt-sleeve and frowns; the ornate cast columns are a spiders' paradise. The front wall is a tapestry of brick in cream and brown. He pauses at the door, a single panel of red glass etched in a flowery diamond pattern. He leans closer and fumbles with the cards in his pocket. The card backs have the same pattern as the glass. He shakes his head; this thing definitely getting to him.

He stares down at his desert boots on the bluestone door-step and remembers the police appearing after a phone call from Don's girlfriend in 1997. Don was dead, killed in a freak accident. The policewoman had stood on the office step right here and held a crumpled piece of paper taken from Don's shirt pocket: Michael's name, the office phone number, address, and the time of their afternoon meeting; the last time he saw Don alive.

Michael had answered yes. He did know Don and had seen him on the day of the accident. No, he was not family, but she did say where Don was found, another odd coincidence with Michael knowing the place so well. The policewoman had raised her eyebrows as if expecting more, then tucked Don's note back in her jacket pocket. Michael inspects the heavy-panelled door, ruined by remnants of Clive's hot pink patch-up paint. The door knocker is a tarnished brass ring the size of a dinner plate, and the doorknob is a cast of Joan of Arc's head.

At his office desk, Michael mulls things over, Maria's take on Don's cards and the imminent arrival of the boxes full of Don's notes - the thought of the young writer's death still too raw for friends and family to deal with after all these years. Michael spreads the cards on his desk and gazes out the pokey window past the monstera to the tram terminus.

He thinks back to his first meeting with the now-dead writer in 1990 Peru, on a steep and narrow path perched on a vertical cliff face. Michael had been shocked at seeing anyone so early and way out there, Don with dirty sandaled feet hanging over the abyss, his young face in a cloud that stank of marijuana.

Michael is apprehensive but beguiled by a dead writer with a surprise connection from the start. He now knows in his heart he took the easy way out back then, the whole thing at a dead end due to too many unknowns until now. He has a distracted weekend at home with his wife, Jennifer.

| 2 |

Early Monday, Michael is outside the office again. He shrugs, oddly hesitant. Inside he holds his nose. The sour stench of cats' pee wafts from the hallway, along with the ubiquitous stink of Clive's stale Gauloises and a dash of mould from an ancient Axminster carpet. Michael knows Don's boxes of notes have arrived, even before finding the delivery docket with Clive's signature shakey but sure.

He escapes the hallway to the front room and shuts the door behind him. He stands at his desk, pulls the pressed metal card case from his vest pocket, and drops it by the delivery docket. He squints and wonders why Clive had been there on the weekend, his old boss supposedly `retired'.

So, the boxes are real. Don's girlfriend Maricielo had spoken of Don's writing, presenting Michael with a handful of pages before the funeral. But he had doubted the boxes even existed back then. He sits, stares at the signed docket between his fingers, and remembers Clive working full-time back then, the perennial frayed tweed jacket and unmistakable Andy Warhol bouffant less gey than now. Clive was curious at the notion of a wandering young writer in beat-up leather sandals and a long way from home. And then there was Don's eccentric French mother, Clive the consummate Francophile, although never travelling anywhere due to a chronic fear of flying. He had been visibly disappointed when Michael dropped the whole thing after the funeral, tucking the cards away for safekeeping and doing his best to forget them.

Back in the hallway, Michael finally follows his nose, the stench of stale cat pee stronger with every step. He hesitates outside the back room. The smell seeps under the door, the loose doorknob cold on his fingers. He pauses before entering and gazes further down the hall to a lean-to roof over a linoleum-floored room masquerading as a kitchen. He finally pushes the door open. With no windows, he gags.

The seven boxes are on the floor, crowding Clive's long-defunct water cooler. Michael stands frozen and inspects each one. The room is gloomy, the two nearest boxes the worst and covered with mildew. He stares at the ceiling, the single light globe dim, bare but frosted. His nose twitches, and he exhales loudly, the bulb beginning to sway and Michael grateful for a gaping crack in the back wall.

One box is on the verge of collapse, and Michael grabs a handful of Don's notes. He holds his nose and covers his mouth, the loose sheets writ in graphite pencil, a heavy hand with a distinctive slant up and to the left. The notes have the occasional heading: a date and place name. Michael shakes his head, the greying curls across one eye. He feels uneasy rummaging through the first of the boxes and reading the sheet on top. He remembers Robbo's call the week before. "Yep, like reading a dead man's diary Mike. I still can't bloody do it."

But Michael too feels very much like the intruder, Don's writing a reminder of how little he knew of the man. But now he has inherited the boxes, and this handful of notes is a window to a teenage Don who had left Fremantle, his mother, and a younger sister, then gone north to make money and see the world.

• February 1986 / Goldfields, WA

On the main road there's not much happening, empty since late afternoon, everyone else at work or trying to catch some shut eye under clap trap air conditioners that shake & shudder. Dogs doze on warm morning tar after barking all night, toothy grins, ragged twitching ears with bits missing, shifting by midday to flop under shady verandahs, the sun high, the sky endless, the occasional truck breaking the spell, the rumble & rattle of a diesel exhaust. The dogs grimace, but barely move.

My digs are tiny, a better cabin than most, a single bunk & wardrobe, a small table for scribbling, an almost empty bar fridge. There's a shared bathroom, fresh bed linen & towels each week, an aircon on the wall above my head, all rattles and hums on paper thin walls, like it's about to come apart. I turn it off & scribble away, or lay listening to Maricielo's Spanish tapes, the masculine & the feminine, the nouns, proper & improper. The words take me somewhere else, the cabin temp rising on hot days, the crusher's thud better than an iffy aircon.

My neighbour is another bloke, grey whiskers in the wash basin, gold wedding ring left by the tap. I hear the door latch, the shower, the stream of water, the clatter of soap that falls to the floor. Outside, a white plastic chair has a cracked arm. At day's end it's about the camp cat. He's got the chair & the last of the sun, curled up & fast asleep. My real neighbour is a fluffy fat tabby with short broken whiskers.

There's always stories, from I don't know where, all dumped in a Mixmaster & scrambled up, me thinking of school, primary school, my best friend a black kid with a shiny steel brace on her right leg, leather strap around a skinny knee, another round her ankle. Gracie runs & runs, as hard as she can, one foot dragged behind, smears her cheeks with streaks of white clay.

Tonight I sit on my bunk, open the tin case & shuffle Mama's cards, the stories I know, the brown velvet edges, the missing corners & creases. There's a hint of Mama's lavender soap, thin white fingers through raven black hair. She pokes at her treasured tortoiseshell combe, the familiar whisper soft in my ear - *Oui*, this card is a boy, relaxed, nonchalant, the feathers in the hair and eyes to the sky, wooden staff slung over the right shoulder. The jacket, it is open, tied at the waist with a piece of rope. & the white tunic is underneath, like the bathing suit in one piece, the leggings knee to ankle. The feet are bare. & we know of course the meaning. *Oui*, another step ahead, but we never achieve the end. Our story, no matter how hard we try, it is never over.

• March 1986 / Goldfields, WA

The empty bar has worn carpet, threadbare hessian, stinks of sweat, cigarette smoke & beer, the barman bleary eyed & staring. The stories rush in, a stone thrown in a millpond, first a ripple, then a torrent, the barman from the Spanish Maine, a shaved head & pirate earring, every story a glimpse of somewhere else, something seen from the corner of my eye.

The pirate scoffs when I order sars. I study his face, no expression & no neck. I see a family in the big city, a chunky kid, a middleclass single mum who tries but can't stand the tats on his thick teenage neck & bare brown arms. Doesn't understand the swearing and road rage but blames his father, a father who's at work or down the pub. There's one brother, self-made with a fancy car, a dolly bird sister with a baby in blue, a cherub with cherry red cheeks.

Yeah, I hear you Siss, but really, these stories, I'm not in control, like an errant supermarket trolley that bounces from one wall to another. They crowd my head Siss, have nowhere to go & just burst out – Listen Brother, get a freakin grip, forget these fairy tales, shape up & move on. Forget the stuff Mother's planted in your dizzy damn head.

Maybe it does come from Mama. There's always been stories, a story every night, Mama on a crochet cushion in her favourite chair, bread in the oven, white skin smelling of lavender soap. Always poking at that tortoiseshell combe, her black hair long, strait as, black kaftan down to the floor, black shawl & words wavering, whispers rising & falling like a chant on a breeze.

Sometimes I wonder if I live in a time machine, drifting & wavering between stories, between worlds, periods & places, one foot here & one foot there. Maybe I live in two bodies.

Once upon a time in France, Mama says, dragons are common, one a wild, toothy beast with a giant tail, shaggy red fur & ungodly stench that stalks the countryside in search of kids to eat. But Mama is all over the place, that story unfinished, another of white-skinned women, Gallic beauties in long flowing gowns, hiding by narrow forest pathways in the darkest valleys. Travellers must dance before they can pass.

But no Siss, it's not all about her these days, me a long way from home, a long way from Mama, this outback town a dustbowl, flea-bitten dogs, shops boarded-up, broken posts & awnings, a general store, petrol pump & pub, less people in town than here at the mining camp.

The rows of cabins are holding pens for drifting in & out, a raised & covered walkway for the rain that never comes. Most use a common bathroom & laundry at one end, the kitchen & dining central, a small lounge & games room out back. The TV hums, grease and cigarette smoke in drifts from a half open door.

The storeroom is a dusty gym, busy at the oddest hours. I hear someone inside, a big bloke with hefty shoulders layered in sweat, a worker from a water drilling company, on the treadmill at 2 each morning. Or maybe a gym junkie social worker, a Marvel superhero, a Viking god, a musclebound

Hulk with green skin & a torn yellow singlet far too big. Like me, he can't sleep through an entire night.

& it's funny, about sleep I mean, the things that come to mind when doped up or drowsy, another girl at school, asleep in class after missing for days. She's locked in a cupboard at home, fed water through a striped straw poked in the side of the cupboard, punished for not making her bed, or changing the channel and dropping the remote on the floor. Comes to school like nothing's happened, steals her stepfather's cigarettes & swaps them for sandwiches.

I sit in my cabin & listen to the stories, the dull thud of the mine crusher, tell myself I need the money, need the dough to get on with life.

***

Michael lifts his eyes from Don's notes on his desk and takes the pressed metal case from his vest pocket. The cards rattle inside. He runs a finger over the lid, embossed with the finest chequered pattern, and a tiny cross in the centre: something he had missed at first but not his old boss Clive, picking up the case for closer inspection. "Nice." He had slowly turned it over. "I see. `Dubois', French of course." He was not so impressed with the cards themselves though. "Just cards Kiddo. And not much colour." Michael does miss his old boss from time to time, although he would never admit it. He lifts off the metal lid and fiddles with the cards like a set of worry beads. He squints, acutely aware of not opening the press metal case for twenty-two years, although it was never quite forgotten.

| 3 |

Michael gazes out the office window to the University and street lights a hazy golden yellow. He screws up his nose at the hint of cat pee on his fingers and wonders if these are all Don's notes. It dawns on him that he will never really know. He shuffles the notes he has from one side of the desk to the other. Some sheets are unreadable, impossibly stained, or completely blank. He drops those to the floor, sorting the others into separate groups. He needs a sensible sequence, stacking Don's notes in piles that mean something.

• February 1987 / Goldfields, WA

I need more dough, a change of shifts, the kitchen night crew sacked, dead drunk & causing grief. After a week, I sit, roll a spliff & take a puff, daylight streaming through my cabin window. Clouds of dope waft around, a card on the floor between my feet, this single card somehow escaping Mama's tin case & now laying picture up.

Mama looks worried. She's always worried. Brushes black

hair from black lipstick lips, face & hands impossibly pale. She clutches a black shawl pulled over rakish shoulders, her words afloat those lavender drifts – *Oui*, this card is the tower, besieged in a raging tempest under shredded grey clouds on a bleak & black sky. Bolts of lightning sizzle & blind, the smoke & flame exploding from a broken roof. Windows too spew fire, a man & woman falling head first, mouths wide & fingers like claws, torn clothes streaming behind. So, here we have the jolt of understanding, the change not expected.

In the morning there's a local bloke watching, Kelvin his name, something that strikes a chord from day one, a jolt from the past, me a Freo kid with stories I barely remember, broken Blackfellas in chains, standing stooped, sullen & quiet, all in a row & against a wall.

There's a nod from Kelvin like he knows me, says nothing for a while, leans on a post & puffs on a rollie, smells of dust & BO. He's half caste this bloke, 50/50 but it's hard to tell. The shirt's open & I can't help staring, these scars across his chest. He waves a fly from the corner of his mouth – Yeah Cuz, mixed blood, but a drop as good as a river I reckon.

He stares at my face, like he's looking for something – Not from round here Cuz? Anyway, got a smoke?

Blokes linger outside the kitchen, standing, smoking, chewing the fat, laughing, looking sideways now & then, but I can't hear what they're saying. Kelvin's eyes are slits & I must look puzzled – Whitefellas, all Newcomers to us mob.

One wanders this way, wide shoulders, baggy blue jeans, bulging belly over a silver belt buckle with a big gold star. He stares at me, then Kelvin, spits on the ground & grinds a boot heel in the dirt. I ask if that's really necessary, get a scowl & a push. He's made his point & goes back to his mates.

Kelvin looks up from the ground & I flick him a rollie. He takes a drag, inhales, blows a cloud of smoke & turns – Some history there Cuz.

I ask why. His eyes scan the horizon, a distant dumped truck & tumble down shed, then back at me. There's a sideways, downward glance – That fella, no time for our mob I reckon.

***

Michael rubs his eyes and ponders all he does know: Don's movements in 1990, their first meeting on a Peruvian cliff face: pencil in hand, a boyish face, that odd blue shirt with buttoned epaulettes, and an incongruous pair of worn-out sandals. And there was a second meeting days later in a lodge above Machu Picchu.

He mulls over the thought of Don rushing home from Peru to his own mother's funeral, then Don seeking him out two years later in 1992 - their first Melbourne meeting - Don arriving late, the radio with news of a chemical tank farm explosion west of the city. He recalls the café crowded, Don stinking of marijuana, and no reaction to Michael's delayed commiserations regarding the young writer's dead mother. The conversation was stilted like always, Michael grateful for the comings and goings of a lunchtime crowd and the fragmented mentions of France and Peru. There was nothing said of Maricielo or Don's hometown of Fremantle.

Michael recalls Don pulling out a crumpled map in that café - not of West Australia, but of here in the state of Victoria, an inkblot mark in the centre of the old goldfields north of Melbourne. Michael frowns. That at least makes sense now: Don had sought him out for a reason. There was something he needed, and it always had been about that Aboriginal connection.

Now it really is late, and Michael squints. Luckily his wife is at her sister's place. He slumps at his desk, his stomach rumbles and he lusts after Maria's chocolate eggplant cake, pignoli cookies, and focaccias ready to go, all that tempered by the impossible task ahead, Don's resurrected cards, and now these boxes of Don's notes. Michael knows he needs to break this thing into smaller pieces to get anywhere.

| 4 |

There is the clang of a morning tram as it changes direction at the terminus outside. Michael stands at his office desk and stretches his arms to the ceiling. The thought of the stench in the backroom is daunting, and his mind wanders. The last time he saw Don was in 1997, their second and last Melbourne meeting. Clive was still working full-time, the young writer finding Michael busy with a private commission, Clive's cathedral project: a tricky family history centred on a Melbourne stonemason and the bicentennial of what remains an iconic city cathedral.

Their very last meeting is burned into Michael's brain, the cathedral an impressive Gothic-Romanesque mix from 13th Century France. There was the French connection again, something Michael's old boss was keen to remind him of.

Like in Peru, then the Melbourne café meeting, Michael made small talk while standing outside: the architect's main spire was not tall enough for the Catholic movers and shakers of the day, the bishop demanding an extra five metres on top. Don's face was typically distant, but Michael sensed a sneer and thought the young writer could do with some sleep. "Don't worry, Mike, a shocker of a nightmare last night, but probably the best I've been for a long while and much better since getting rid of the dope. Siss never happy, of course, still complains. Says I read too much."

Michael recalls the smell once inside the cathedral - old paper and dust - and a mass of work to wade through. There were the paintings, photographs, sketches, and extravagant costumes. Open, heavy-clad books sat on crowded benches with 19th Century newspaper cuttings, blueprints, and building invoices. Don was soon trailing behind, Michael ploughing through everything he could find and Don with little apparent interest until reaching the mannequins.

Then something had happened. Don seemed stuck like he could go no further, head back and gazing up at tall figures in pearl-encrusted robes, the crimson, silver, gold, and violet, the high hats and golden mitres. Michael watched, the young writer looking small and insignificant, standing stiff, hands deep in pockets. "Yes," he thought, "maybe the mannequins could be intimidating to kids, but adults? Surely not." And yet Don did look ill, his face odd and pasty, standing frozen in the flickering candlelight.

The office back room is stuffy and stinking, with shadowed shapes on mouldy walls. Michael sinks to the floor and kneels, Don's boxes all around. He takes a deep breath as best he can and rubs his eyes and nose. He tallies up the meagre progress so far, with two handfuls of notes processed and all these boxes to get through. He tugs at another box and rubs his calf muscle to relieve the pins and needles. He stretches the leg, brushes the greying fringe from his forehead, and pushes another box aside to make space; the cardboard is soggy, bulging, giving way and collapsing. Several sheets of Don's notes glide over the rest and flutter to a stop. He stares at the top page, a tingle at the back of his neck like a mild electric shock, the scrawl already familiar, the leaning text, this header placing Don in 1997, the very year of their final meeting and the horrific accident that followed.

| 5 |

• May 1997/Goldfields, Vic

I'm under the verandah of my house in the bush, drag my foot on leaf littered rock. Flurries of early snow, thick possum skin cloaks warming strong shoulders, lifelong stories in every cloak. Finally rid of the dope I've a sense of direction. I'll return Michael's books, grab some writing stuff, some new sandals & fuel. & that means money, a casual kitchen stint somewhere near The Albert Hotel.

• June 1997/Goldfields, Vic

Inside the house I rummage about, stack stuff away, jamb the door shut & close up. But no one's coming all the way out here. I march down the hill, one trip enough, a box of my latest scribbles for Robbo to store, a water bottle, change of clothes, beans, nuts & dunny paper. I pull scrub clear of the bonnet & load up, give Gracie a push & jump in, roll down the hill until the engine kicks in, head for the old coach road, hardly notice the village, my mind already back at The Albert.

Robbo. Heaps to catch up with, knows me as good anyone. His wife Anne too, but she won't be keen to see another box of my scribbles in their garage. There's Michael to meet on the same day, his books & my silly questions about Blackfella stuff up this way. There's that new book to pick up at The Theosophical Society, the answers out there, now I know what to look for. & there's a flight back to Freo, to meet Dad & chew things over, now that I've finally been here.

OK Siss, I see your screwed up eyes, & that pout, but you only know half the story – Come on Brother, because you told me nothing! Don't you dare give that bastard the time of day, not after how he treated us. Remember? He left us. & all this other stuff? Bullshit the lot of it. & really, take a look at yourself Brother, skinny as a rake, a dead man walking. & get yourself some decent freakin boots.

• June 1997/The Albert, Melbourne Bayside

My first night back, & in the morning it's still dark & I'm suddenly awake after a crazy night, covered in sweat, this narrow iron bed with the covers thrown off. I stare across at the door, bleary eyed, the light through the keyhole, the gap under the door & the passing shadows in the passage outside. I lean over to the table, grab my leather satchel & poke my hand inside for paper. I sure as hell need to scribble this down.

So, I'm asleep in bed, last night's scribbles scattered on the floor & sensing someone's here. Waking, but not waking, butterflies in my stomach. The walls flicker, the patchy paint & dull lights that come & go. I feel hot, the window almost closed, the dull click of traffic lights downstairs, a flutter in the curtains. Next, the bed shudders with me in it. But how could it be, me asleep? There's a vibration through the wooden floor, the thumps from the bed legs like a machine gun, a clatter & bang from the table. There's the smell of smoke, the air thick. I'm thinking this is stupid, no dope for months, me asleep but not asleep.

Then, there she is, this vision morphing from somewhere near the wardrobe, then standing by the bed, bolt upright. Her face is round, innocent, plain Jane features, alabaster skin but something not right, her black hair scrappy & cropped real short, a face so serious for someone so young. But the eyes are angry, fearful, defiant, just a kid this girl, her white neck small & slender, crooked slightly forward, her gaze levelled directly at me.

But I don't know what she wants, don't want to know, that extended right arm thin & pale, skinny as, a small hand reaching from the folds of a dark hanging sleeve, palm facing me, fingers parted, nails ragged, rough & broken. I feel I could touch her, stretch out & press my palm against hers.

The long dress melts around her body, a rope belt at her waist, dark blue folds down boyish hips & thighs. I imagine thin legs, small white feet rooted in fresh air, the smoke & shadows, the floor black & wet. There's something plaintive, overwhelming & urgent. She doesn't move but her eyes do, sideways from the window, back to me, like there's somehow a way out from where we are. But it's weird, this kid so familiar.

And now it's me that can't move, my time machine locked in the eye of some storm. I just don't know when it ended, now nothing & the room still dark, me suddenly scribbling the whole lot down though, all I remember, a dull strip of light streaming through the gap in the curtains, & that girl, she's not Mama or you Siss. I remind myself it's just a dream, but the lamp lay on the floor.

& there it is right on que, today's bout of sisterly advice – Oh Brother dear, & you tell me everything is sorted, when Mama's freakin French fairytales are still alive & kicking. Don't worry, Siss is here.

| 6 |

Michael drags his eyes away from what are Don's final notes. He is not comfortable, but this is ridiculous. There are even the odd tingles on the back of his neck, and he puts it down to the date at the top of the pages and meeting Don for the last time the very next day. He stares at his reflection in the office window. He has no way of knowing if the dream was real or just another story. But then, even if it was a dream, it probably meant nothing. And yet, Don had looked drained and oddly unsettled inside the cathedral at that final meeting, and there was an obvious disdain in the young writer's voice as they left. "Sorry, it just bothers me Mike." He had stopped mid-stride and stared into Michael's face, those brown eyes glaring. "I mean, that excessive wealth, that self-righteous preaching, and the politics. It just makes me physically sick. I've no time for it, not in France or South America and certainly not here."

There was no time for Michael to answer back then, with Don on a mission: returning Michael's borrowed books but collecting another at The Theosophical Society. "It's not far Mike." Michael nodded. Clive's precious cathedral job could wait. They crossed the road by the parliament buildings and headed down the hill towards the city. Michael was curious about Don's map from their last meeting at the café. "Yeah Mike, still got it. Finally found Grandad's country, by the way. So, thanks for that." The young writer's face took on a red flush. "It's true. It was Dad who first told me about Grandad being over here. He gave me the map, marked a village smack in the middle of the old goldfields. But really, there wasn't much to build on, and yeah, it was you who provided the spark I guess, back in Peru. Oh, and your books of course."

Michael turns to the office bookcase and Don's borrowed books still there, sitting at one end and covered in dust. He taps on the desk, then the pile of Don's notes. Yes, that last meeting does bother him: walking from the cathedral to The Theosophical Society and sitting outside on the steps, Don thumbing through pages of his newly bought book, Michael staring across the stream of car bonnets and a forest of parking meters.

He had always expected more from Don, their brief meetings and conversations always seeming unfinished, and this time Michael left alone on the Society Building steps, dropping the two returned books in his briefcase. He had stood to stretch his legs, his foot kicking the small pressed metal case - Don's cards left behind. Michael had shaken his head and bent down to pick it up among the roar of motors and car fumes. The cards stirred inside, along with the metallic rattle of what was Don's gold neck chain. He abruptly stood up and turned as the traffic lights changed, with Don out of sight and no chance of catching him.

Michael poked the unopened case in his vest pocket for

safekeeping, to return to Don as soon as possible, not knowing that this time the young writer was gone for good.

| 7 |

Michael checks his watch, bothered at the thought of his wife waiting at home and already annoyed on the phone. He pushes Don's notes to the side of his desk and stares at Jennifer's shopping list. He remembers her studying Corporate Law when they met and Jennifer's father blaming Michael for wrecking a promising career, neglecting his Princess, and being an all-round disappointment. He hated Michael calling her 'Jen'. Michael stares out the window, across the road, and remembers her at University. She was a year younger but taller, her red hair a storm; a cool customer with that private school accent, skin delicate and pale, but self-conscious of the freckles across the bridge of her nose.

His eyes are drawn back to the notes, and he thumbs through the latest pile and takes a deep breath. Clive still says Michael tries too hard and worries about doing things `properly' all the time, and never sees the big picture. Michael says Clive looks for things that are not there and imagines his old boss at his desk, blowing smoke rings and pondering his unknown unknowns. Michael shakes his head and focuses on the job at hand, the last of this unsorted pile on his desk. He labours through the pages one by one and does his best to ignore the stink. Don has left Fremantle and gone north as suggested by his best friend Robbo.

• August 1986 / Goldfields, WA

A construction bloke passes through camp, a bit quiet until one day he opens up. He's a welder by trade, always smiling, but not quite right I'm thinking, no teeth & a persistent cough, a voice loaded with gravel, a face all hair & elephant leather, a white weal of a scar beneath his left eye. He props outside by the kitchen door, his chin on his chest. It's early, the laboured breath soured by booze, him wanting to chat about stuff. He asks if I travel much. I mention Maricielo, but what can I say? He winks, a sly smile – Aye me Boyo, there's always the black haired beauties.

I look away, but there's no stopping him – Me? Been everywhere I reckon, Belize, Bahrain & Kazakhstan.

I guess they're countries, or cities maybe, & he nods – Well me Boyo, you're a youngster. There's so many places to see, & a big wide world of black haired beauties.

The words are slurred & he points to his hip pocket, grimy & torn – There's good dosh too, 'specially in the production plants & offshore platforms, all the fuckin money you could ever need.

He grins & spits – & me Boyo, that'll take you away from dumps like this clapped out mine, with its cracked, fucked up cooler piping.

Yeah, he has been everywhere, both hands with tattooed

knuckles. & I wonder. Does he know my best friend Robbo? Again, his mouth narrows, a toothless grin – Aye, bet I fuckin do. But you know what? There's a bit too much Red Heart rum under the bridge in here.

He taps the side of his head with index finger that must surely be broken – Memory's not so good these days. Come to think of it, me liver's pretty shot too.

Now I'm staring at his right ear, can't help it, a row of studs that dance in the light, & an ancient hairy earlobe. He fumbles the studs between thumb & gnarled finger, not too drunk to notice me looking – This me Boyo, is one snazzy piece of handiwork, don't you reckon? Cost me an arm & a fuckin leg.

He nods – Yeah, thousands!

But I'm not sure what the point is, & he's sussed me out straight away, cackles, narrowed eyes suddenly aglow. He shakes his head, points a tattooed finger in my face – Well, for what else other than the black haired beauties? They love the fuckin sparklers!

But suddenly there's a change, his face all serious, the smile gone, a creased frown on a weary sunburnt brow & eyes half closed in the midday sun – To be honest me Boyo, these days I'm feeling a bit clapped out, a bit old. Aye, can't do what I once did. Need to catch one of them black haired beauties & settle down, before it's too late I reckon.

I turn to take in a horizon of dull red plains, the cool breeze on my face, the patches of scrub all ashimmer in the sun. He normally sleeps on the open tray of his ute he says, somewhere out there, away from the snakes, the scorpions & lizards. But he'd be scraping ice from the windscreen in the morning, so he stays in the camp for now – Too fuckin cold I reckon. No good for old bones.

| 8 |

• April 1986 / Goldfields, WA

The camp manager has ogling eyes that dart here & there, a crooked limp, wanders the kitchen & helps out from time to time, his veggies overcooked, fruit salads soggy & always with a hint of onion. A rollie dangles from the corner of thin grey lips that quiver when he talks, the blokes whinging about ash on the tables & dinner plates.

I see him, a young emigre like Mama I suppose, her own baggage from France, him from the north of England, his limping leg from a mine shaft accident a kilometre or more down, an ore trolley flying off its rails and pinning him against a cut. He gathers his savings, ends up here, a partner in an accommodation & catering outfit. He struggles to breathe, emphysema he says, admits he's lucky to be alive. I hear him coughing & retching in the night.

The dining room has long trestle tables, a jungle of plastic chairs. I look across the servery, the sea of changing faces, most solitary, minding their own business. Some are escapees like me. Yeah Siss, that's what you'd say.

Then there's the sociable types jabbering about this & that, stuff that doesn't matter one iota. There's Stumpy, Cookie & Johnno. There's Blakey, Bugger & Brownie, no real names here. I help with breakfasts, check the vegemite, stock the table for the day & night shifts, make sure the onion chopping board is nowhere near the fruit. After breakfast there's a deaf & dumb conga, workers packing their lunches in silence for wherever they go. One packs peanut butter sandwiches, white bread every single day. With the sinking sun they return like bats, covered in grime, insidious & black, the smell all dust & sweat. They sit through an entire evening meal, again in dead silence, most melting away to the communal washroom, then the lonesome solace of their cabins for the night.

On Fridays, some make their way to the pub up the road, the blokes a mix, the shy & the cocky, heaps of excuses why they're away from families or friends. Others don't care & don't make an effort. Yeah Siss, like me, not much of a joiner.

The pub's a dive, windows shuttered, the inside stuffy & loud, loaded with BO, beer & more sweat, the blokes in blue, grey & khaki. Cigarette smoke hangs in layers, a cob-webbed ceiling caked in grime. I've no interest in small talk, fast cars, football or girls. I just don't get it. Siss says I should get out more – Snap out of it Brother, drop the freakin fairy tales, take an interest in real life, join the human race.

So I go once, a fight to the bar & a platinum blonde with green eyes, her head above an ocean of hats, wide & peaked. She's one of 3 barmaids from Kal. I push closer, the place impossibly packed. She asks what I want, bare brown arms pulling beers, jiggling white tits with golden tassels. Words from somewhere else. I step back & turn away, dissolve in the crowd & escape out back, the carpark cold and dark, the street light broken, gravel grinds underfoot. Yeah Siss, that's me, the back door as usual.

Around the camp I see vacant eyes everywhere, opportunities lost, love, life, families & friends all somewhere else, missed birthdays, anniversaries, kids growing up & that first day at school. I wonder, about those empty eyes.

There's this young couple working long hours in camp & kitchen. They look happy enough, not like the others. Maybe it can work, unlike with Mama & Dad. Sometimes they wander at night, to get some air they say. She's always glowing, excited, saving money for a city wedding when they go back home, with 7 bridesmaids she says. & there'll be lots of kids. He's quiet, sort of smiles & looks away. I think of Maricielo, wonder why I'm bothering.

Yeah Siss, I know what you're thinking. But I promised & here I am, with my Spanish tapes & a satchel full of chicken scratchings. & I know you Siss, watching over my every move like you always do, these days with too much makeup, bleached hair, shaking your head & jangling jewellery. I say my scribbling makes things real, so I know where I've been & where I'm going. But yeah, I know they all wonder about the stories. Like you Siss. They shake their heads, nod, a sideways look in my direction.

There's a bloke from the nightshift, always looks worried, a tall woman with a straight back & sad eyes at home, a worrying wife that wonders about a husband who doesn't know what he wants, & how he'll ever fit back into her world. She's a strong woman that one, an independent type, like you Siss, Mama too.

& yeah, I know it was tough for you Mama, being an artist, the material world a necessary evil to make ends meet, selling the occasional pottery piece, some sewing & crochet – *Oui*, but there is nothing I would not do for you, like in this card. Look here, closer, this one an old man, the emperor, wise & weathered, serious with a long white beard. & here, a gold crown that shimmers, the robe hanging heavy & open, his armour of silver. He sits on a grand throne wrought of stone, the left hand grips a globe , tee square in his right. So, sometimes, *oui*, it is the material that rules, sometimes the necessity.

This bloke's got 3 kids & an Irish Setter puppy that jumps the back fence, says he gives his family everything, all the money they need, & nothing but the best. But I see an empty house for sale, a neglected garden of scraggly hydrangea, old person blue, a note in a pink envelope, smudges in one corner, a hint of jasmine perfume more honeyed than sweet. Life's lonely it says, him never home. She'll leave before the month's out. I see a grown man silent but crying, a single tear dribbling down, whisky breath, a trembling bottom lip & chin unshaven.

I sit & scribble, the aircon flicked off for some peace & quiet. But now it's freezing. I repeat simple Spanish phrases over & over, shiver & stare at the window fogging up, the bars outside, my finger cold & wet, Maricielo's name with a question mark. There's the opening & shutting of the adjoining bathroom door, the dull thump of the mine crusher, the real world somewhere outside.

***

Michael scratches his chin; by now, the stench of Don's notes going nowhere. There is the rattle and clang of the occasional tram reversing. Michael lifts his head and stares out the window through the trees to the lights of the University. He squints and brushes an unruly lock of hair from his eye. He is increasingly uncomfortable being dragged along by this thing, pulled along, fumbling with Don's cards and wading through the young writer's water-stained, rancid notes. Michael shakes his head. "Jen will be ropeable, getting home at this hour, and without the shopping."

| 9 |

Michael's dinner is predictably cold, Jennifer stony-faced; first, the cards are back, now these boxes and the endless hours in the office. And there is family trouble to add to the mix, Jennifer with a flight booked to Queensland in two days' time, her brother and father fighting again. Michael squints, like the bad old days when Jennifer's brother smashed the family car with no apology in 1997. Michael baulks at the thought of another coincidence: 1997 being the same year Don was killed in that crazy accident, Jennifer travelling north with the twins - just nine years old back then - and Michael flying to West Australia for Don's funeral. This time the older brother has lost everything in a dubious bitcoin deal.

In the morning, Jennifer is preoccupied with her trip, and Michael surprises Maria early. She rolls her eyes, and he sips his coffee. The same cards lay on the table in their metal case, his thoughts lost in Don's boxes, and the current batch of notes on his office desk.

• March 1987 / Goldfields, WA

Kelvin comes & goes, between the mine & town camps. He's got more stories than even me, a smile slow & broken, big on teaching the kids – Stories? Need 'em to keep youngfellas strong & out of trouble Cuz.

& there's something else that twigs, a link between us, me always scribbling. Kelvin scratches his chin, twists his mouth in concentration & nods – Like our stories but different.

There's no mucking around with Kelvin, just needs a bit of time. No small talk, no agenda, not out to impress this way or that – Must pick own path Cuz, the signs always there.

Kelvin talks of great snakes that open up wide red lands, talks of totems, songlines, skin clan, rules & sacred places, country holding bad things in, punishment for wrongs done – Gettin in with wrong mob, no good.

I notice other Blackfellas about town, skin real dark, some with jobs like Kelvin, but all come & go, their voices a babble, eyes downcast at first, some with broken English like Kelvin, many with none at all, long quiet spells, no words but lots said, important things, names that can't be spoken.

Kelvin has a nephew, skinny, self conscious & quiet, lives in a humpy on the edge of town, finds a wrecked rust bucket of a car left by some construction rigger, resurrects the wreck with bits & pieces from who knows where. The engine kicks over, splutters to life & rust rimmed wheels roll, this kid only 10.

I see a strength that has to be. Still here despite it all, a strength to match the leanness of the land & all that's thrown at these Blackfellas. There's a young bloke & his wife, from a desert mob to the south east. I see a small baby in tow, a runny nose, the buzz of flies, a round black face. They hope to sell boomerangs & other stuff for mine workers' kids, walk 500k from their country to this, bare feet, slow steps on sand, spinifex & rock.

• May 1987 / Goldfields, WA

Can't sleep again, need a breath of air & leave the camp through the hotel carpark. There's a mob drinking round midday, by the old diesel pump, what's left of a garage wall, a flag & faded words on brown brick – Welcome to The Lucky Country.

There's movement in the shade, the smell of stale beer & piss, a twisted figure in a dried up drain, plastic bottles, broken glass & wine boxes busted, a big woman moaning, legs splayed out from the knees, bare feet like plates covered in dust. She's sobbing this woman, her breath catching, floral dress grubby, stained crimson from neck to waist, black face bloodied. Before work I catch Kelvin outside the kitchen, passing through he says – Yeah Cuz, things gettin bad when old ways forgot.

His face is close to mine – Got a smoke Cuz?

Those eyes narrow, warm tobacco breath, raspy voice – It's poison that spreads. In the cities, young brothers' eyes are blank, the same as their souls. There's sniffin the petrol, breathin the glue, Newcomer greed, the grog & them drugs.

Kelvin shrugs, the most chatty he's been – In the past we fix 'em Cuz. Guide 'em to a safe place, dry country 'ere, hot, trees makin shadows in a fryin sun.

I feel things changing like flicking a switch, but there you are Siss – You & your stories Brother, out of the frying pan & into the fire, a fairy tale a freakin fairy tale in my book.

| 10 |

This card, *oui*, the angel, feathered wings wide & curly golden hair. She trumpets to the earthbound from billowing white clouds. Below are every man, woman & child. Each answer the call standing with arms outspread, rising from open coffins afloat the turbulent sea. *Oui*, it is knowledge we seek.

Kelvin is the teacher, asks me out on country & there's no roads where we go. The camp truck's seen better days, the dawn light faded & washed. He stares ahead from the passenger seat – Yeah, about learnin Cuz. Watchin, then dancin, knowin bout the land & old people.

He stops, like he's thinking, clears his throat – In the beginnin there's each animal, then the ancestors, the Big Fella Spirit, the shaker, diggin & shiftin dirt.

Further on we stand by the truck, Kelvin's eyes skyward, more endless blue. He kneels down, one finger in red dust, knows his people, their footprints, siblings & relatives, some not seen for a year or more, taps the side of his head – I know

41

this one Cuz, Uncle Eric for sure, seein the signs, a bush broken, a mark in the dirt right `ere.

Kelvin takes two steps, spots something, freezes in his tracks, tugs at my shirt sleeve & points to the shade of a dry river bank – See 'im Cuz?

But my eyes see nothing, Kelvin insistent, his tug more urgent, drags me aside – You be careful Cuz, 'im called the walk around snake, up & huntin, nasty fella that one.

Back at the truck, there's a smudge by some spinifex & it is not all about snakes. Kelvin stares for a minute or so, nods – Animals movin on secret lines, secret burrows & 'oles. Dirt moved 'ere. This fella a big one. Not so good though, hurt foot. If we get hungry, we follow 'im Cuz.

Kelvin stands, stares at me, waiting, a narrow toothy smile, amused at the thought of a vego like me, out & about in Blackfella country.

Another week & we're at the rainbow cliffs mid morning, leave the truck & walk, our path a creek bed, eroded, all stones & scattered scrub. Kelvin stops just ahead, a pillar of rock blocking our path. Something else I don't see, not at first, this painted figure small, standing, bolt upright, a black silhouette on yellow rock, headdress like an American Indian, both hands raised high & wide. Kelvin motions me to be still, finger to his mouth, then shouts out 5 times. Getting permission, he says. I follow when he beckons, the hum of heat in the air & the whistle of a faraway kite. I feel the stare of a lone crow watching.

The first paintings are off to the side, down an ancient gully, a rock overhang low & cool, Kelvin reaching up, almost touching hands that float mid air, red silhouettes, some splayed with extra fingers – See 'em Cuz? There, & over there. Old Fella paintings.

I see them alright, but Kelvin moves on, slowly, slowly. Wouldn't see a thing without him, the 'roos, the goannas, the turtles & floating fishes – This one 'ere Cuz, the dreamin story, my people & the animals, Big Fella Creator Spirit bringin life to everythin all round.

He props on one leg at gully's end, the air cool but dusty. He points, at odd images I don't get, like nothing I've seen before, painted flying bodies, clay spacemen with bulbous heads, halos, hollow black eyes & no mouths. Kelvin whispers, one hand on my shoulder, stares at the ledge above us – Ah, so you see 'em Cuz? These spirits. Much magic, power too, no need for mouths these fellas.

It's another week, on another track I can't see. The truck exhaust all rumbles & rattles, diesel fumes through Kelvin's window & we finally stop. Here are more pictures in coloured clays, the browns, the reds & yellows – Special colours 'ere Cuz, special clay from old days. If we don't 'ave 'em, we trade 'em.

At the cliffs Kelvin points, a shallow cave up high, more stories, more secrets. We climb, all shale, red dust & feet slipping, sharp stones in my sandals. Kelvin's up front, bare feet broad, the cave opening low & dark, cool air on my face from somewhere within. I duck my head, can't see a thing, turn & shade my eyes, the endless glare already hot. I wipe my brow, peer inside, my eyes adjusting – Show you somethin Cuz, waitin just 'ere. My mob's place, my totem.

I glance around & shapes appear, bleached bones of small animals a pile in one corner. Kelvin sits, legs crossed, breath low & soft, me on my bum with legs out straight. I lose track of time till it comes over dark & I wonder what's happening. He taps me on the shoulder & I jump, the cave opening blocked, a giant bird suspended on the slightest breeze, just hanging there, head turned to me, eagle eyes focussed & fierce, flight feathers curved upward. Then he's gone like he was never there, the endless view back, the red shadows ashimmer, the clumps of yellow a spinifex sea.

Back at camp we sit outside the kitchen – Got a smoke Cuz?

Kelvin blows smoke rings, raises one arm, his hand tracing the horizon – All our country Cuz, long time now, all them cliffs & rocks. & you seen 'em Cuz, under them trees all along the riverbeds, the creeks with water deep down. Old Blackfellas allover, in the hills, desert country too. Remember 'em Cuz.

He shuffles, eyes narrow, seems restless – But the other stuff Cuz, all sorry business, them buildings out there not belongin & not 'ere for long. Newcomer stuff.

Kelvin is missing in action more often than not these days, me in the truck to ruined leftovers of failed farms, land that showed promise once upon a time. There's this homestead, the house paddock a salt pan, a windmill toppled & on the ground. I take a swig of water & prop in the verandah shade, the buzz of bush flies & something dead beneath the floor. Inside are family portraits on crooked walls, pasty pictures of bearded men, faces all serious, black hats & braces. Women are decked out in sunhats & long frocks, all white with frills, a once black bible on a dusty bench.

Out back there's an iron shack with no windows, dirt

floor, freezing cold in winter, but good for Blackfellas. I see a tall bloke at the door with bad news, a rifle, wide brimmed hat, woollen suit of the drabbest grey, baggy jacket & pants. A woman answers, younger, face black, upset eyes, dress white with high collar, long sleeves & hem, a small kid between them not 5 years old.

I turn away. Don't know what it means, never do, wander across to the shearing shed, a once grand dance hall now deserted. I listen & wait for the echoes to come, of footsteps on dry wooden floors, the air thick with the stink of greasy wool, the oddest squeaks & rattles, the creak of pulleys, scuffs & stomps that bounce off rusted walls. It's the dance of wiry shearers, balls of muscle in dirty boots, the shouts of bragging, the impossible tallies, rushing tarboys like blue arsed flies. & swayback sheep, wide eyed, the whine of cutters, the indignant bleats.

Suddenly all is quiet, my time machine again, one hand on the top rail, dust between finger & thumb. I listen to my own breathing, shallow, the scuff of my sandals, drive shafts above rusted & bent, sagging belts still, a death shroud of dust & cobwebs.

Outside I peer under the floor, through broken battens, a netherworld, dark & cool, earthy air that hits my face, tottering timber posts, crazy angles in sheep shit dunes.

I wander, yeah, don't I know it Siss. There's a door to the bunkhouse on 3 broken hinges propped open & gaping. Inside are lonely long gone names scratched in parched planks & posts, welcome shelter from sweltering heat & wild, willy willy winds.

The dust up my nose makes me sneeze. Pages from

magazines flutter on the wall, once glossy, all tits & big hair, Amazons in saucy swimsuits, bodies draped across car bonnets, others propped on motorbikes with leather seats that look too big, the silver studs in shiny rows, more girls on the timber floor.

Back at camp I sit outside, stare up at the Saucepan & Southern Cross, line up The Pointers & look north, Kelvin's world the entire sky – Much more up there Cuz, Big Fella Emu, The Warrior just there.

His eyes narrow – Got a smoke Cuz?

There's a half nicotine smile, shaggy head dropped, chin on chest. I wonder what's brewing, if he'll ask me where I've been. He spits in the dirt, eyes again skyward – The early days? Don't remember much Cuz. Me just a Blackfella kid, me sister, she's older. Don't remember seein Dad. Just Mum, & a dingo pup, sandy colour, small. Cheeky that fella.

Kelvin sniffs, shrugs, drags on the smoke & spits again – I remember Cuz, them Newcomers, late one night, boots stompin, big hats, missionary fellas. Sayin nothin, yankin my arm. That little dog, bit a fella's ankle, a kick for 'is trouble. They grab Mum so she can't move, her shoutin to run like hell & hide. They get me sister though. But I know where I come from, know my people Cuz, Dad's people, & Mum's goin way back.

That's the most he's ever said, stares at me like he's waiting for me to say something, gazes around like suddenly remembering where he is, then back up at the sky – Mum, she always says 'bout that Warrior fella up there, if we on country & see 'im Cuz, we kids up too late & should be 'ome in bed.

| 11 |

• March 1988 / Goldfields, WA

There's so much stuff I just don't get, all this info & where it comes from, everything connected, the land, the family, the weather & those that came before. It's just that Kelvin knows so much, like a computer, speaks 4 languages, never been to school, no need for a fancy house or car & all that Newcomer stuff.

On Sunday Kelvin just sits there & I wait until he wants to chat – Bad business Cuz, this fella from our mob, runnin off, me goin to special law country.

He had waved me away, his clenched mouth & worried eyes an imprint on my brain. Flat on my bunk I can't sleep, floating high above, light a spliff & stare down from the stars to red dirt & outcrop rocks, a steep escarpment on 3 sides. I follow Kelvin, his head & shoulders, his purposeful stride, head looking this way & that. Finally, he stops, the clearing a circle of dirt, red coals that glow on a centre fire, the smell of spinifex, pungent & thick. I watch Kelvin sit face to the fire, see his bloodshot eyes, feel the air still, the gloom engulfing, the yowl of a dingo, distant & forlorn.

At first there's only Kelvin, but then he has company, a hunched shape opposite that tends the fire. He's a scrawny one, shoulders sharp, whiskered face long & thin. I imagine a glint in his eyes, focussed on his hands then on the coals, mumbles to himself. Then I see it, the bone in his hands like it's floating, a stick or a nail, straight & pointed, held flat in his left hand. Now he's dead still, waits, seems to glare. I drag my eyes to other shapes, more men on the edge of the circle, 6 in all, from the old bloke an even split to left & right. 2 approach the fire, shoes & masks made of feathers.

I close my eyes, alone up here, surrounded by stars, asleep but not asleep. I sense a tremble in the old bloke's voice, soft at first, the breathing circular, a chant from the others, Kelvin too, a murmur, a drone. They wait, that wrinkled right hand with the bone real tight, wedged between 2 rakish fingers, the old bloke's black face blank, eyes that stare, flames aflicker. Those fingers trace the bone's full length, slow at first, then a race to the end, suddenly at the point. I hear Kelvin catch his breath. The old bloke's right arm jerks, straight, abrupt & urgent, fingers & bone that point to the dark. The fire cracks, the 2 dancers right there, their stomping an echo off unseen cliffs, the old bloke still, a blob in the darkness & I wonder if he's awake.

I shiver on my bunk, fumble with Mama's tin card case in my pocket, a world far from here, lose myself in the thought of soft card edges & the pictures I know. But now there's this stuff, something I know but don't know, thinking about those dancers in special slippers that leave no track, feathers fixed with blood, taking the bone to point, the job done, that wrong now right.

| **12** |

I reach for the cards. 1, 2, 3, deal the fourth, missing corners, edges soft & brown, backs stained, the pictures faded. Mama says I get stuck between the positive & negative, need to steer my way through – *Oui*, like this card, the horseless cart with 2 wheels, the man in armour, shining silver breastplate & helmet, standing tall, strong & in total control, his surrounding world of castles & towers.

When I was a kid, Mama seemed sort of in control. Then came the cards & I wondered. & now maybe there's something that makes more sense. But Siss waves her finger, bracelet jangling – Fairy tales? Dreamtime? Can't you see there's no freakin difference?

The blokes call Kelvin a bludger, lazy black bastard, typical they say, not reliable, too much time on his hands. Like me Siss. This time he's had it up to here, Kelvin gone for good. & still they complain. Didn't even say goodbye.

With Kelvin gone I'm on my own, take another card off the top of the pack – An angel sits on billowing clouds, eyes closed, arms wide, the wings strong. She is crowned by the sun. The man & woman are lovers & face each other from opposite sides. The man looks to the woman, the woman to the angel above, an apple tree behind, a coiled snake around a tall straight trunk. *Oui*, these lovers are our balancing act.

Ah OK, relationships & partners. Yeah, I know Siss. You're shaking your head again – Oh Brother, that tart really does have you by the freakin balls.

If you say so Siss. & I can't say I've forgotten, a little black dress, the patchouli perfume, wide eyes, wild hair, black like Mama's, the boozy breath & soggy rollies with lipstick tips, tits that bounce when she throws her arms about. But really Siss, I just don't know, there's a big world out there.

I reach across to my bunkside table, the piles of scribbles & Maricielo's letters from a world she wants me to see. She's changed, keen when she never was before, the letters insistent, me having a go at Spanish, the drone of her tapes rolling, the monotone maze of phrasing, the nouns, the masculine & feminine, sleep never an option, sun streaming through bent bars, the words taking me somewhere else. Yeah Siss, there was the sex, but don't ask me what it's all about.

***

Michael has waded through another pile of Don's notes, more unreadable sheets on the office floor. He wonders about the glow of his desk lamp, passers-by peering in and moving on, knowing nothing of this pressed metal case in his vest pocket, or the backroom boxes that stink to high heaven. He takes a deep breath, pulls himself up from the chair, stands and yawns.

In the backroom, he squeezes past Clive's beloved, long-dead water cooler and drops down on his knees among the boxes. He knows more than he did the first time around – twenty-two years ago – the accident and funeral leaving too many questions to sort back then. Now he has Don's personal take on things, just eighteen when he leaves home and heads north. And again, long-forgotten thoughts of his own life flash through his tired brain: Michael is a country kid as Clive reminds him, a young boy playing footy with the mission kids. He remembers their dirty feet bare, black faces daubed with white streaks of clay.

The boxes crowd Michael, every page another story, like peeking through a newly found window. He has trouble with what is real and imagined, ponders his piles of loose ends, and sifts through another box; Don is working through his own puzzle, his heart set on France. And Michael gets that; loose ends that gnaw and needing answers to move on. Not that Michael always follows his own rules, having swept this thing under the carpet after Don's funeral all those years ago.

| 13 |

So, I'm finally here. Mama's country? Northern forests, old people from once upon a time, the moss so green, great trees standing & those already fallen, the reds & yellows of the leaves, a richness in the soil. & there is something else I just don't get, the smell of fire in this haven of green. Yeah Siss, I know – There you go again, seeing things that are not freakin there.

But I do see things Siss, everywhere, ancient ways, vibrations in the dirt, paths hidden & half hidden, before the cities, the battles & wars. This remnant of a forest was once endless, taking months to hike through oceans of beech, the oak & spruce, the chestnut & elm, a gloom so foreign, too dangerous & foreboding for civilized folk.

& here, Mama's Freo stories return, of a wizard imprisoned, a fountain of youth, a sorceress enticing unfaithful youths. Just here a sorry business, stands of trees & souls of women that die in childbirth. Harming a tree is the worst thing, to damage the bark of the Earth Mother's elm, the

53

wrongdoer cut open & gizzards wound around the trunk. I lean back, stare up, the branches a canopy loaded with green & this spliff all done. & I have the cards.

Bees & butterflies mob this lavender hedge, the cards spread on sprawling green grass, each in the shade except one that's lit by a shaft of sun – *Oui*, this picture a fearsome beast, the background black as night. He roosts on a high rectangular pillar, the perching feet clawed, a bare barrel chest & bat wings, the face a frown with wild cat eyes. The head is crowned with a pentagram, large pointed ears & a sweeping pair of goat horns. His right hand is raised, palm outwards, the other down by his side holding a flaming torch upside down. & look here on the ground in front, a man & woman to both sides, both shackled to the beast's pedestal with a sagging chain, each with Puck horns & tail. *Oui*, this card is clear. It is the card of blindness & misconception, a lack of light or understanding.

But I don't get it. Not really. So is there something here I actually don't see?

• September 1989/ Rennes, France

OK, so why am I here? Well Siss, it's like this. It was about Mama & me, & about France. Or so I always thought, about trying to explain why I'm the way I am. & where's it got me? I've been sick as a dog, I mean real fucking sick, the weeks gone & me still here, next stop Peru. But I can see her, Mama in Freo, her favourite chair, shaking her head & staring out the window, worried eyes & whiffs of lavender, hair long, shining & straight, the whispers in French – *Oui*, but I worry about this plan of yours, not wanting you to come & getting so very sick.

& then there's you Siss, always with everything sorted, waving your finger – Hate to say it Brother, but I told you so, that freakin France stuff all made up. Just knew it would end in tears. Even Mother didn't want you to go. A waste of time & money in my book, to say nothing of letting yourself get sick & not having a clue where you are. & then, as if that doesn't take the cake, making some stupid freakin promise to that tart in South America.

| 14 |

Jennifer is not impressed with Michael's late nights at the office. And these boxes are the last straw; with breakfast a silent affair, her preoccupied with today's Queensland flight to smooth things over between her father and brother. Michael stares at the table, and she pouts, dabs on the last of her lipstick, fiddles with her pearl necklace, and sighs. He drops her case and overnight bag by the front door. These days her hair is grey with splashes of red, the goodbye kiss more of a peck and nothing further said. Michael shakes his head, thinking: "I just hope the old man's reasonable this time around. God knows I don't need his shit with these boxes dropped in my lap."

The cab outside is ready to go, and Michael is left with Jennifer's untouched jasmine tea. After all these years, he worries about giving her father more ammunition and can see him waving his finger in front of her face: "Told you so Princess, should have aimed higher. Great kids though, all grown up with proper jobs. Every bit of it down to you."

Michael still feels anything he does is not good enough. He recalls his father-in-law not happy with Clive's job offer back in the eighties and demanding Michael get a real job.

But, like Jennifer's father, Clive also was ambitious, not even fifty back then and already with a financial package from the University. Michael was in his early twenties and only a year after marrying. He smiles at the thought of first meeting Clive at a pub: The Prince Hotel a triple-storey building with a corner bar and a Ladies' Lounge. That lounge was Clive's favourite haunt, always at his best with an audience of eager students and assorted academic hopefuls.

Michael empties Jennifer's cold jasmine tea down the sink and recalls Clive's formal job offer. The twins were just babies; Clive's typed note with the letters 'l' and 'i' indistinguishable thanks to the worn-out keys of an antique Triumph typewriter. His new business ranged from small-time University research to family genealogy. Clive had heard of Michael's PhD, his paper on the Ancient Greeks.

Jennifer had worried at first; her father's opinions were never far away. She had laughed at those flourishes of French with the exaggerated accent. But Michael was never fooled by the eccentric professor act. With a frown and screwed-up nose, Jennifer took some convincing.

Michael sighs, always in awe of Clive's good luck, inheriting his 'new' office from his spinster aunt, along with her typewriter and water cooler, the place ideally positioned and a short stroll from the train, the University, and of course, The Prince.

Michael remembers Clive's big break like yesterday, that opportunity thanks to his University friend Adele: feisty and French, an orange Thai scarf flicked from one shoulder to the other when making a point, and The Prince Hotel crowded. Clive was listening for a change, the air thick and smoky, high wall shelves loaded with empty glasses and ashtrays, Clive dragging on one Gauloises after another. Adele had spruiked the Federal Government's cultural-based policies and a convenient expansion of current arts grants. And she knew an anthropologist in South America; the first Michael had heard of Jean-Paul, The Frenchman.

A flurry of activity had followed, their phone calls, emails, and bourgeoning plans, Michael's first job seeming to grow around him, and with two new babies.

Then there was the unsatisfactory finale, Michael returning from Peru and neatly packing everything away after the funeral, leaving Clive disappointed and Jennifer doubtful that Michael could move on.

But now the empty house is silent, and Michael's thoughts drift to the office, this thing back with a vengeance thanks to a bunch of bulging boxes, Don somehow immortal, and the *déjà vu* of Jennifer in Queensland again, just as she was at the time of the funeral.

| 15 |

Michael arrives at the office around midday, already tired. In the backroom, he sinks to the floor, Don's boxes all around. He tallies up the progress so far, almost a boxful read, some notes making sense and others not. He pulls another box towards him. A further batch of pages lay on the carpet, the stink catching in his throat. He stretches a leg and brushes the greying fringe from his forehead. Michael pushes that box aside, suddenly conscious of the years gone. The twins are all grown up now; Clive's Peru Project almost thirty years ago. Michael was a newbie back then, working with The Frenchman, an Internationally-respected anthropologist: Clive's plan for them to be there for almost a month.

Michael recalls their first goal, the two men reaching the mountain top and temple ruins in the dark and The Frenchman's headtorch shining on his notebook. Michael was impressed with the three-metre granite panels, placed vertically to catch and reflect the first rays of the sun. And he wanted some time alone, heading down a narrow cliff-face path for a better look at the vertical panels from the east, until turning a corner and being startled at meeting Don for the first time.

He recalls catching his foot on something, his way forward

blocked and the young writer's backpack open, Don just sitting there in semi-darkness, the feeble beam of a torch light and the crow of a rooster somewhere below. Up close, there was that blank stare, the forever boyish face under clouds of smoke reeking of marijuana. And Don's shirt seemed odd right from the start, smart casual and out of kilter, pale blue with buttoned-down epaulettes on both shoulders. The pants were slacks, and a pair of sandals hung over the abyss. Michael has not forgotten the fear, feeling paralysed and one step away from certain death; his flashing thoughts only of Jennifer and the twins.

Alone in the office backroom, Michael is propped on one elbow among Don's boxes, his gaze drifting from the cracks in the wall to one box after the other, then settling on the floor and one page in particular. The heading at the top is disconcerting, with thoughts of that cliff face and Don's detached expression. Michael rubs the back of his neck. There had not been a single word exchanged, and he squints, eyes glued to the page header, the place and date: a dead man's perspective on that same first meeting. He is again uncomfortable at the thought of being led. He drags his legs from one side to the other and thumbs through this batch of notes.

| 16 |

· **November 1990 / Ollantaytambo, Peru**

I climb the steps, follow the track down, across the face
of the cliff & find a spot wide enough to sit, the ruins way
above, the sun about to rise & light up the mountain. Yeah,
Siss, I know, not the safest place to sit scribbling after hiking
up here in the dark. But here I am, & there'll be no tourists as
silly as me, or that's what I think.

My satchel is bursting, full of scribbles & pulled from my
pack. I roll a spliff, puff away & pry open the pressed metal
box. I know each card by heart, every picture, the browns &
reds, the soft edges, the creases & missing corners.

Funny, this bloke strutting down the track, me not seeing
or hearing him until he's right on top of me, an older bloke
in desert boots with curly messed up hair. He stops & stares,
almost falls over the edge, wants to go around me but turns
back. I throw my stuff together & escape further down the
track. Yeah Siss, running away again

Away from the ruins, there's peace & quiet on another
ledge. I scribble in the early light, another spliff, another time

& another story. This time it's me, I see myself. I'm hiking along this ledge with a heavy load on my back. I stop for a rest, on top of the world. On one side a wall up to the heavens, smooth like glass & impossible to climb, the other side a chasm. The path in the story is my path, faces circling with hollow black eyes, pale faces with no mouths. I look around, roll another spliff. If I fall, I'll float until rescued, lifted up & carried back to this ledge, settling here with my load, my cards & scribbles. But now the town below is waking, lights winking, matchbox houses with Medieval walls, terracotta roofs, stone gateways & narrow streets. The air laced with floral tones of lavender hedges that remind me of Mama.

The top card is face up, a ragged rider on a rearing horse – *Oui*, a jaundiced skeleton, white headband with trailing tails, the long handle scythe clenched in both bony hands, the blade curved & cruel, unholy hollowed eyes in a fierce face. Frightened figures cower from the horse's prancing hooves. On the ground lay butchered body parts all about, the certain fate of pontiffs, kings & queens, mother & child.

So, I know there must be a transformation, a change. Is that change Maricielo? Well, I'm here now, but not sure where I want to be, second guessing outcomes & dreading failure, tell myself changes are healthy, shouldn't wait for stuff to just happen. & then there's you Siss, steady as a rock, screwing up your nose & apologizing for your older brother's loopy behaviour – Brother? Yeah, I've told him, a strange bird that one, talks to himself you know, imaginary freakin friends from when he was a kid.

| 17 |

Michael rubs his eyes, leaves the office, and drives across the river on his way home, with a head full of Don's notes and no enthusiasm for an empty house. He turns off and down the road near where Don was killed, parks the car by the squash courts and turns off the radio. His squash-playing days are long gone, but he remembers the day after the accident and the call from Maricielo like yesterday, the police revealing the location and him knowing the area so well: the girls' school next door, the golf course, and an asphalt path in between.

He now realizes he had been in shock after the news, had left his old Holden where he is now parked and wandered in a daze, drifting to the golf course fence. He must have turned, then followed the school wall to the end of the path and a set of traffic lights. He clearly remembers the last pair of trees, the end of an avenue, the traffic lights and the peak hour traffic stopped; across the road a synagogue with its great green dome, the exhaust fumes and sky so grey. Twenty-two years later, he is in the same carpark, staring out the windscreen to the squash court walls, having gone over this repeatedly in his head so many times.

Don had disappeared that fateful night, leaving best friend

Robbo, passing the synagogue and walking this way to The Albert Hotel. Had he waited for the little green man and audible clicks to cross safely at the lights? Or had Don not bothered waiting, turning back briefly to gaze at the huge looming dome, then crossing the road regardless? There surely would have been next to no traffic at midnight.

Michael winds down the car window for some air, and again re-imagines Don crossing the road halfway home to his hotel. But Don strays from the path to take a pee – too much sarsaparilla – the shadows darkest by the school wall, shrubs and elm suckers up to his knees. The air would have been earthy and damp, those brown eyes and face so boyish. Michael shakes his head. His visit after the accident had resolved nothing, standing there alone after work, gazing across at the red brick wall of the girls' school, the last flecks of sun a motley maze, the flash of traffic lights off to his side, the sudden clamour of rush hour mayhem.

It is over twenty years ago, but Michael is still surprised at his selective memory, not certain about how he got to those last two trees exactly. And yet he clearly recalls the killer branch laying broken and bleeding, certainly big enough to maim a man, but cut in pieces and dragged aside. He recalls just standing there among the twigs and leaf litter, the wet grass, the car fumes and the sweet scent of sawdust. He had finally turned, drawn to the actual trunk, his hand raised to the still-wet stump, the red sap oozing from the chainsaw cut.

Today Michael stays in the car and stares at his reflection on the windscreen. He notes the wrinkles and his greying curls, shuffles in his seat, the car park deserted, and Don's cards a lump in his vest pocket. The feeling of being stuck is back. He still wonders after all this time: What if Don had not strayed towards the school and in the direct path of the falling branch, or turned at the lights and walked alongside the main road? What if he had crossed further along, avoiding the path between the avenue of trees? If only he had been five seconds earlier, or five seconds later.

The policewoman on the office step had summed it up: "In the wrong place at the wrong time." Michael squints. "Mmmm. Like his mother, but neither accident suspicious." Don was killed at midnight with no one about, the exact time pending the post-mortem. He would have felt nothing, or so the policewoman said. But Michael still wonders how she would have known.

Michael just sits there with his hands on the steering wheel and his thoughts of the tree. After twenty-two years he has no enthusiasm to see it again if, in fact, it is still there. He remembers the wounded trunk, his eyes dropping to the ground, a red flower and note at the base of the tree. Michael had bent down, the flower a West Australian kangaroo paw and the note wet, on plain white paper, the writing bold with a now-familiar upward slant.

And Michael still has the note, gazing around the empty car park and pulling the paper from his pocket, the message from Don's distraught father, smudged and almost unreadable, resurrected from Michael's sock drawer, along with Don's cards. The words are blurred and broken by blobs of red sap but remembered word for word. "Finally found your country," the note signed 'Dad.' Michael tucks the letter away again and gazes in the general direction of the tree.

He stares at his hands, white knuckles on the black

steering wheel. And an odd thought grips him: Like Don may not really be dead, the young writer in hibernation for over twenty years and waiting for someone to decipher the notes in the boxes and finish one last story.

Only Don is dead. Michael had seen the actual tree back then, the trunk and bark, the ridges a wrinkled grey, standing there with an elm leaf in his hand, serrated and coarse like sandpaper. He recalled the other leaves all around, a melded mix of green, some light, some dark. Another month and the path would be smothered by a thick carpet of rotting browns and yellows, the smell more intense, earthy, and wet, with First World complaints from dog walkers and joggers, the slippery path dangerous.

The thought of Don lying there still bothers Michael the most, a young man crushed in his prime, the ground damp in the dead of night, Michael standing there at the very tree just days later, unnaturally cold to the bone, staring at the note from Don's father, the cards a bulge in his vest pocket like now.

| **18** |

Michael is back in the office first thing. He cannot leave Don's notes alone but even now still feels uncomfortable peering into the young writer's innermost thoughts. His hand is in his vest pocket, the cards a permanent fixture since rescuing them from the sock drawer. But his thoughts still dwell on the killer tree, Don's notes from France, the tree references, quaint folk tales, and an arborist friend's matter-of-fact appraisal of what had happened that night. Michael pulls out the arborist's folder from twenty-two years ago, blows off the dust, flicks the cover, and remembers his friend's frown. "Elm trees? Sure, known for strength. It's the twisted texture and the spiral nature of the grain."

Jeff the arborist had paused. They had not seen each other since University and Michael was a family man with two young twins back then. Jeff asked after Jennifer and quickly realized this was no gardening issue. "Yeah, the elm, been around for a long, long time, about forty million years." He had waited, but Michael wanted more.

"Well, Mike, bigger elms in Europe and North America, they're really something, difficult to cut and split." Only when

Jeff ran out of steam did Michael mention the accident. Jeff nodded. "Ah, so that's it Mike. Whereabouts?"

Michael heard nothing for a day, meeting Jeff at Maria's for coffee. "Well Mike, you can shut the book on that one; no black magic there. The limb failed under its own weight, the branch seventeen metres long with a low horizontal habit, your tree almost a hundred years old." But Michael did not get it back then, a tree renowned for great strength but suddenly demoted, collapsing in still conditions with no wind or warning.

Jeff had nodded. "Well Mike, it's like this: there was heavy rain the day before the accident but little rainfall throughout the previous spring, summer, or autumn. Anyway, we call it 'sudden branch drop syndrome.' Look, it makes absolute sense Mike, with the tree stressed over time. The branch collapsed under the additional weight due to the recent rain and sudden water intake. In short: the lower branches have grown far too long as the tree sought more light, extra leaves generated at the end of the branch and the trunk join subject to that extra stress."

Michael has the boxes now, and it bothers him even more: the thought of him and Don on the steps of the Theosophical Society, a random tree dropping a killer branch that very night, Michael at home with Jennifer, and the twins just kids. He had kissed them both goodnight and poked his head outside, the air cold and clear, the night mist dropping, the front lawn wet and the grass newly cut. He recalls Jennifer's Chanel No5 filling the bedroom, her alabaster skin, and that stunning red hair a storm on the pillow. He had lain awake for hours that night; something was not right.

He stares out the office window, squints, drops the arborist's folder back in the drawer, and shuffles Don's notes. He gazes across at the University gate, the fleeting traffic, the morning sun on street trees - every one an elm. He squirms in his seat, head spinning with the thought of a loud crack in the dead of night, the branch breaking around midnight, the school wall black, the dank smell of dead leaves, the echo like a rifle shot with only Don to hear.

| 19 |

The drive home to an empty house is another blank for Michael, and yet here he is. His thoughts are full of trees, all those years somehow gone, and just lately the headaches. Jennifer is in no doubt; the culprit is the ridiculous hours and lousy light in Clive's dump of an office. Michael drops his briefcase and car keys on the hallstand at the door and throws his jacket on the floor. The room is dark, and the TV is on with the volume down. A lone street lamp shines through a gap in the curtains. There is the thump of a car on the estate speed hump outside. At some stage, he stretches out on the couch, the room awash with greys and blues, Michael immersed in the realms of late-night news and the state of the world, the flash and fade on living room walls. He turns to the screen, neck twisted, eyes more closed than open.

He yawns. The world has gone mad while the Amazon burns, a president with yellow hair and orange skin, impeached but not defeated. Villages are bombed, and homes are blasted and burned to the ground. Tents float on a sea of mud. There are church bombings, mosque shootings, bloody-minded blockades with millions starving, an upturned boat, and body bags on a pebbly beach. Suddenly he is wide awake, a young reporter on the screen, the words' mouthed.

Michael rubs his tired eyes and squints, sees a familiar boyish face and tan, Don's wide brown eyes and the open-neck business shirt with epaulettes. He imagines a fine gold chain around the young reporter's neck.

Numbers flash across the bottom of a silent screen; refugees, the missing, maimed, and homeless. A million flee and gather at some border, mass graves, murdered families in fields and farmhouses. Michael drags himself off the couch and flicks off the TV. He shrugs, takes a deep breath, and concentrates on what's real, the good things. He is a lucky man with a beautiful home and wife, both kids all grown and with good jobs. And there is finally talk of grandkids. He shakes his head. If only Jennifer could see him wandering around in the dark and talking to himself. But there is no point in trying to sleep.

Michael drifts back to the hallway, picks up his briefcase, and heads to the kitchen. He nods to himself, the house quiet and everything in its place. He runs a hand along the edge of the kitchen bench, props on a stool, and opens his laptop. A soft gong alerts him to a new email, the sender's name transporting Michael back to Clive's Peru Project and The Frenchman's world almost thirty years ago.

| 20 |

The Frenchman's email includes an extract, part of his last commission before retiring and returning to France for good: a Quebec University study of an Indigenous sculpture collection. Michael scratches his head. He has not seen The Frenchman for over thirty years, although speaking regularly on the phone. He wonders if a break from the boxes might be a good thing.

At first, Michael is reminded of The Frenchman poring over that other project, all those years ago: a coastal collection of ancient Peruvian figures, one more grotesque than the others and dressed in an odd feather suit. It sat on its backside bolt upright. Michael squints and recalls the legs stretched out front with large duck feet. He pictures the arms: like sleepwalking, except for the hands twisting like robot claws. But for Michael, it is still about the ferocious head, a space-man helmet mask with a gaping mouth and sharp sabre tooth fangs, inside the mouth a smaller head, the eyes staring, but narrowed and nasty, the nose screwed-up, a pointed bone through the septum. And he recalls The Frenchman back then, a waft of cheap cologne, that already-bald pate, monk-ish with wire-rimmed glasses, an accusing finger in Michael's face: "As I have said many times my friend, there are more things in the world than your bricks and mortar."

Michael sighs, still wondering what human experience sets the scene for creating Peruvian nightmares like those, and these - The Frenchman's latest - crazy inexplicable sculptures from some northern Canadian wasteland and an unknown people. The same intensity and power that bothered him back then are right here, although these are black-and-white pictures. Michael scrolls down through The Frenchman's email. He peers closer and feels challenged by these prehistoric pictures of oddly engraved harpoon heads and knives of chipped stone, bone, ivory, and wood.

This is not the distraction he needs; the images are tortured with stressed spines and ribs. The bodies are pained with twisted tattooed faces. And there are masks with fiendish and toothy fangs or tusks, ringed eyes, and mouths distended as if in agony, their bodies tangled in crazy rites. Michael reads The Frenchman's summation, mouthing the words: "Most certainly shamanistic-inspired my friend, handed down from generation to generation and never to be forgotten."

The silence looms about him, Michael feeling very alone, all in his world not so safe and sure. He needs fresh air and to clear his head. But it is too early for the office, and he stares down the hallway to a linen cupboard door, home to his aging squash racquet and running shoes stuffed in the bottom compartment.

| 21 |

There is no city traffic this early. Michael turns back into the service road and parks his car within sight of the War Memorial. He stares out the passenger window past the nearest street lamp, a sprinkling of light on early morning dew. His eyes are drawn across dark sweeping lawns that roll up the hill to the mausoleum wrought from grey granite. He rubs his eyes and can just make out the distant but familiar smudge of an outline. He knows it well, Classic Greek, those colonnades, the porticoes, and pediments. For Michael, it could be the Parthenon or the Mausoleum of Halicarnassos.

Michael has not run for years. He gazes up at the last of the stars, the bats distracting, the squeal and screech insistent. He leans on the car body, stretches old hamstrings and calf muscles, and steps onto the running track: 'The Tan' being Melbourne's iconic running circuit. He turns north towards the city's lingering night lights.

For Michael, it always was about loose ends and putting the pieces together. And now he has the boxes, surely making this thing no more difficult than a jigsaw. He met Don and Maricielo in Peru, and then there were Don's two Melbourne visits. Michael had high expectations of answers after the accident but left the funeral with too many questions. The stink of the bats reminds him of Don's backroom boxes. He cannot catch his breath and already has a twinge in his knee. His thoughts are all mixed up, with what he had heard and the notes he is reading. And now his old boss is back on the scene, Clive signing for Don's boxes and dropping by unannounced, puffing on his awful Gauloises, the ashtray spilling on the floor like the old days, and Michael left to clean up the mess: "Slowly Kiddo, this your last chance to put the whole thing to rest once and for all."

Michael's footsteps are more like shuffles, the running track of yellow crushed clay. He turns at the river and into the morning light, the clustered row of boatshed gables, Melbourne's river upside-down, brown, and on its way to the bay. There have been headaches, and now his knee. He risks a twisted ankle or worse with the light so dull. Towards the bridge, the track is flat and easier going, and he picks up the pace. He wipes his brow, the hot sweat stinging his eyes.

He shakes his head, Elms everywhere. The shadows are unsettling, crazy shapes trying to tell him something, visions of The Frenchman's latest horror distractions or Don's twisted body sprawled in thick autumn leaf litter, neck and shoulder broken, boyish face pressed to the ground under the killer branch.

Michael squints. "Rows and rows of the things." He mulls over his Melbourne history from before Federation; the course of the river changed, native trees and bush cleared for something more appropriate, the new plantings reflecting a grand European city. And Michael does appreciate good planning, design, and building: his world of bricks and mortar. It bothers him when things don't go to plan or when Clive and The Frenchman's red herrings stop him from sleeping.

Michael stops, gasping for breath with his hands on his hips. He peers around. "More damn elms, as far as the eye can see, imported in the days of sail from across the ocean." Michael raises one hand and stares; these same elm trunks were smaller than his little finger back then.

Finally turning to face the main hill, he grits his teeth, the slope notorious, a five-hundred-metre grind. He takes a deep breath and heads off slow and laborious, the track now a pavement and the perimeter fence of ornate cast iron. His chest is heaving, the peak hour car fumes and a bus is changing gears. Colonies of bellbirds chime from a forest of green; his gasps drowned out but not his thoughts.

| 22 |

Don's boxes lay about the office backroom, Michael rubbing his aching knee and pulling aside the two he has marked with the word 'Peru.' He selects a handful of notes and wanders back to his desk for sorting. The page headings take him back to the temple ruins after that first cliff face meeting thirty years ago. The young writer has disappeared, The Frenchman pottering among the walls. "Well, my friend, not so many tourists with the recent political troubles." Michael had frowned when The Frenchman shook his head. "Someone down there in the dark?" The Frenchman had scratched his chin. "Is this possible?"

Michael admits it was odd, and he was not surprised at The Frenchman's doubts back then, the older man distracted, obsessed with the residue of All Saints' Day: dead relatives leaving their world to visit the living and reinforce links with their children, grandchildren, and great-grandchildren. He recalls the never-ending interviews with Indian families at gravesites, the decorations, their gifts of flowers and amulets, food, cigarettes, and alcohol; The Frenchman in his element and Michael nodding in the right places. But Michael knew what he saw on the cliff face that morning. Don was no ghost.

Michael shuffles Don's notes on his office desk and reaches for Don's cards in his vest pocket, his fingers stalling at the faintly embossed cross on the case. He remembers The Frenchman finally finished with the temple ruins, peering up from his notebook, those wire-rimmed glasses low on his nose, and the constant musing. "So, with the families' gifts, it is only then that the dead, they can return to their graves. They say goodbye until next year. So, you see, my friend, it can sometimes be the dead that guide the living."

• November 1990 / Pacai Mayu, Peru

I've escaped the few tourists with no trail I can see, just the faintest vibes from those that came before, this energy under my feet. So, I somehow know the way, onwards & upwards, avoid the valley campsite & any prying eyes, on to the east, one spur, then another to here.

Time for a fresh spliff, another card & the scent of Mama's lavender soap – Look here, the child with wild golden hair & arms wide. *Oui,* he rides the white horse down a winding road, bathes in the warmth of dancing sunbeams, surrounding sunflowers a reflection of this earth. & the sun is here, above it all, for us the giver of life, at shining face reticent & unchanging.

But something did change, black robed Newcomers with a new God to replace the old, the stone cities impressive but obviously The Devil's work. & I see a gathering, one man taller than the rest, hair shining & platted in braids, uncivilized, eats with his hands, bare shoulders strong & fine woven vest. He frowns at the suggestion that all around is owned by Pope & King, this Newcomer Bible a minor God with small square leaves. But these Newcomers are keen to enlighten, building a great oven with bonfire below, the howls & screams of roasting animals a perfect sample of Hell.

| 23 |

From fort ruins, I stare down on the tourist path, a vacant snaking strip through jungle. Up here it's fleeting clouds, the setting sun low, alpine scrub binding broken stone, over-grown rocky parapets & storm scoured dirt. A crooked cause-way leads to a large pond with water like syrup, silent & brooding, the surrounding plateau of elephant hide.

I throw down my pack, flop on the rock & lean on one elbow. I juggle the cards. The air is wet on my face, whispered voices, ancient & soft. One card beckons & Mama points to a seated woman – You see the face. *Oui*, pallid for one so young, robes from shoulders to feet, a curtain backdrop of eclipses & leaves. A tall pillar stands on either side, one light, one dark. She wears a double peaked hat, pale orb in hand, translucent & cold. A silver cross on her chest, a gold crescent at her feet, on her lap a printed scroll, half hidden but there.

This is the sum of all I know & all I'll ever know, a link between my stories, between you & me Siss, my wants & actions, another crossroad, maybe a precipice. I scribble as always, tuck the sheets in my satchel, the pond my inkwell, poignant & black.

So, my world is in parts, always has been, the summits ragged, the valleys deep. Across the pond a rampart rises, here one second, gone the next, racing clouds that swirl & tumble. Cold air catches my breath. Tiny birds hunt bugs in grassy tussocks, dart through bamboo thickets & dance on broken boulders.

Later it's porridge & beans, the echoes of night birds, wing beats muffled & a black rock backdrop. I light up & listen, one spliff after another, a distant wind through craggy peaks, the sky splashed with stars, survivor sparks that float & shimmer, the almost gone & long gone. I think of Kelvin, his Warrior guide, the old people & the way things were. But he is there & I'm here, this millpond of ink & glass, an astral net, a flat, flying carpet.

Now the whispers are back, won't leave me alone, chants low & muffled. Surrounding faces have half closed eyes, wide foreheads & wild, whiskered chins on chests, & blue blankets wove with red.

With first light it's even colder, bitter even, the air clammy, my feet aching. Can't eat this morning, a strange pull to a shallow grotto, me on hands & knees, tired eyes peering. Small heaps inside are ears of corn, random piled bones, big skulls from old people of a copper sun, before the buildings, before the Newcomers, the world that was & everything in its place.

But now it's a different world, with their fear of being forgotten, this need to make a mark, the buildings grand, reshaping their world to something else, a people losing their way, confused, forgetful, manmade dreams coming apart at the seams & rock walls in ruins.

A single card lay in the dirt by a cold bowl of beans & I peer closer to make out the picture – *Oui*, a woman kneels with right leg bent, her foot in a pool. Her right hand holds an urn that pours water on water. From the other there's an offering for the earth. In the distance a single tree sits all alone, the hills an horizon. Above is a mighty centre star, circled by & another 7.

All will be sorted if I search in the right place, now just days away from Machu Picchu & Maricielo. I pack the tent, the satchel, scribbles & bowl. I chew coca leaves for the altitude, leaving the pond, the ruined round ramparts, past smaller pools in rocky pockets. I drop down to the track, the begonias, swamp & bogs, fuchsias like a spray of blood, orchids in clumps of yellow & pink.

The final passes are few but powerful, vibrations in the souls of my feet, a sorry business that lingers, the moist jungle air colliding with these eastern mountains. I see a father in a striped poncho, face lined, worn out & weathered, shoulders strained, his load a blue plastic bulge bound to his back with coils of rope wrapped about his chest. His feet are wide but bare, the ice like glass, the load slipping & he's caught off balance. He's suddenly gone, pulled over the edge, & lost with no sound.

At night I hear distant wailing, 5 wide eyed kids & wife in a hut full of smoke, the stone doorway dark & low.

• November 1990 / Phuyupatamarca, Peru

I stop & close my eyes, this last pass impossibly narrow & on top of the world. At first there's a jingling, the rhythmic tramping of sandaled feet, relays of caravans bearing gifts from faraway places, from jungle, desert, water & land.

llamas prance with twitching ears, know I'm here, their heads jerking this way & that, their eyes big, pools of black, flickering white lashes long & unreal. Rainbow coloured ribbons fly from long craned necks. The cantankerous animals stop dead & stare, shake shaggy heads, then push on past, bundles stacked high on woolly sway backs. They stamp their feet & spit at their handlers, wild men with coarse voices & pierced noses. Fancy clad emissaries walk tall in alpaca cloaks that brush my legs as they lift their hems to clear the mud. Attendants' feathers are saffron & blue, straight staffs with carved condor heads.

There's the clap of hands from further on, a man on a raised raft, the grunt of porters that gasp as they pass, the smell of sweat on the sparse mountain air. They steer their load away from the edge, this man held high, a gold badge on vicuna vest, a noble cloak with emerald edging, a rainbow headband of macaw & hummingbird, his world the sky & ours the earth.

Suddenly I'm alone, one foot after the other, push through a tunnel, the air warm on my face. Clouds of butterflies crowd the exit, the ground wet from perpetual fog, these cloud forests on the eastern slopes, the rainforest a living thing, a dreaming thing, festooned with vines & Spanish moss. Tree trunks are covered in humus, clumps of cacti, lichens & orchids, with forests of ferns at my feet. Birds cross from jungle & valley, feathers that dazzle the senses, mixed flocks with flashes of yellow, black mantle & back, humming-birds impossibly small, a flycatcher grey & quick, finches with short cone bills. In the shadows are bears.

I dump my pack, sit for a while & turn my face to the mountain wind. More stories. Me in this time machine that melds & morphs, Newcomers arriving, now smugglers, gunrunners & bootleggers, miners, thugs & fortune hunters. They all arrive & leave.

Other ways are blurred, unseen & overgrown, connecting places that were always there, good, bad & indifferent. Just here I sense a meeting of paths, a wandering scarecrow tall & thin, another Newcomer. But this one roams alone, his long coat black with human bone buttons, a hooked nose, small cruel eyes & thin white beard. He comes & goes with each ill wind, calls out with a raspy voice, chases down women & kids, kills & collects the blood for distilling & running the government's machines.

In the morning I breathe easier, settled among these skyborne ruins, unseen among the clouds & terraces, the constant murmur from ritual baths, water on stone, pond to pond & down the valley. The porridge is cold & thick, another journey almost ended, me not keen on tourist trails, taking them to where they think they need to go. But for now, that trail is my trail, a night at the lodge, Maricielo like I promised, then Machu Picchu. I still see her letters at the mine, piled by my bunk, me wondering what the hell to do, whether to come & what's it all about, the drone of the mine always there, the aircon's rattle & hum, the thump of the crusher day & night.

| 24 |

Michael and The Frenchman had arrived at the lodge late. Michael was excited at the thought of Machu Picchu the next day but keen to catch up with the latest from home with the twins just kids back then. The call to Jennifer was unanswered, and Michael made a note to try again later. He recalls their guide Paco setting up camp and the almost-empty barn of a central hall, the travellers' bar, and additional wings for basic accommodation. Low music crackled, barely an echo from a cassette player tucked under the bench and smoke hung in lazy layers that stung Michael's eyes. He thought the barman not long out of school with a moustache wispy and thin.

Michael first spied The Frenchman at a small round table, his notebook unusually closed and those wire-rimmed glasses low on his nose. Across the table was a young woman - Maricielo - Don's girlfriend. Michael shakes his head and remembers that second meeting well, Maricielo in her mid-twenties and more the Goth back then, the plum lipstick and jet-black hair down to her waist. Don had appeared from the bar, and Michael observed the young writer approach, the same neat casual look in contrast to the ratty sandals and grubby feet. Up close, there was no sign of recognition on that boyish face that Michael could see. He was conscious of staring as Don sunk to his seat, then squirmed, and tugged at his shirt top pocket: surely the bulge of his mother's cards.

Michael was suddenly aware of Maricielo talking, her smile awkward. "*Si*, it is always the greed and the *corrupción* that bothers me, but now I see the extremes for what they are in my country. Both these sides, they become the same." She had raised her arms to form a circle. "The left and right, they come together, somehow."

He feels it more acutely now, being dragged along, meeting Don on the cliff face in the middle of nowhere at some ungodly hour. Then meeting again at the lodge above Machu Picchu only days later and with time to observe Don in detail. He could tell Don was Australian, although hesitant and softly spoken.

Michael smiles to himself. The young writer had mistaken The Frenchman for an archaeologist, Michael's colleague with those steel-grey eyes unnerving and wide behind his glasses. "No, no. I am certainly not, and if I can offer an opinion here, it is not so much about the archaeologists and their precious buildings. Many, they are simply drunks, a miracle how they can perform a proper day's work. Me? I am an anthropologist, *oui*, with the tools to look further, beyond the obvious." His eyes settled on Michael ever so briefly. "I tell you my friends, these archaeologists; they are bricklayers and wreckers. No, we must never look to them for all the answers."

Michael was struck with Don and Maricielo just sitting

there, waiting, The Frenchman pushing his glasses up onto the bridge of his nose. "Now... for our business, you are wondering, and I shall tell you. It is human history, the journey, and the can of worms we are calling civilization. *Oui*, I am thinking some people, like our good friends the archaeologists, they are preoccupied with the classic notion of their Old World. There are, in fact, many worlds."

Michael stares out the office window recalling Clive and The Frenchman over the years: remembering their gentle jibes about his PhD on the achievements of his Ancient Greeks. Some things never change. But then, without that, there would have been no job with Clive, no Frenchman, no Peru Project, and no Don, his cards or boxes.

The Frenchman was not quite finished though, swigging his water bottle and sitting it on the table. "*Oui*, these archaeologists, they cannot tell us what happened here at Machu Picchu for example, about the actual end of things. Was it wild jungle tribes arriving some moonless night, finding the whole place already empty and having no use for walls and buildings? Do I see them returning to the jungle as quickly as they arrived, leaving the city silent and deserted for centuries? As I say it is only the buildings these archaeologists ever see, the pyramids, Pompeii, Cappadocia, and the Colossus of Rhodes. All these places, *oui*, they are products of civilizations, but me, I see people, with the same dreams as us, the same fears. I hear their stories." Michael can still see Don nodding his head.

And still, The Frenchman continued. "So, my friends, here we are. At the gates of the city, with no writing, no wheel, mummified bodies in the shadows, magic, and mysteries everywhere. And this is not unique, for, on the other side of the world, there is again no writing, the longest continual civilization in the world: Australia. No mean achievement, *oui?*" The Frenchman had tapped Michael on the shoulder and was gone. He had the day's work to compile and record. With The Frenchman gone, Michael felt Don seemed to lose interest, fidgeting with the card case in his bulging shirt pocket and eyes that wandered. Michael remembers a full bottle of wine, a sudden whispered message from the barman and Don rushing away and leaving Maricielo alone with Michael for the first time.

Michael taps his office desk with his fingers and shuffles Don's notes. Some float from his desk to the floor, all these memories flashing through his head.

| 25 |

At the end of another long day, Michael stands at his desk to stretch his legs, the old embarrassment returning as he recalls that drunken night at the lodge. He knew his words had rambled at best, boring Maricielo about Jennifer and the twins until the slurred conversation drifted back to the young writer himself.

Don's girlfriend had shrugged. "Don? You will get nothing from this man, not so much the talker. You see it tonight, out the back door with no word. But I shall tell you something. He does not think of the consequences, enjoys being alone I think, running from the crowds. He is here, but I am not sure it is for me. Do I worry? *Si!* He is not so prepared, too few clothes and a little *loco*. He takes the risks, his tent light to carry, but so small and the fabric thin. And you see the open footwear he has, the simple huarache leather sandals, the cuts on his feet, the dirty bandaids, this a test I am thinking, with the mountains cold, and the rain."

"Back in Fremantle, Michael, I am different, drunk often in those days." She had suddenly stopped and rolled her eyes. "Haha, *si,* even worse than now Michael, smoking many joints, boys too. I am busy saving the world my father says; my mother's daughter. The truth is I am selfish then, thinking I am so clever, quoting poetry and knowing everything. So, I don't see Don in the beginning, then one day I am sober, must make him notice, and it happens. Sometimes his guard, it is down, and I hear stories of his mother, his old cards with the pictures. But I never guess what he thinks."

Michael knew nothing of Don's mother or the cards, not back then, Maricielo's hazel eyes unnerving, staring down at the lodge table top, finger and thumb grasping the short stem of her wine glass. "My father, he hugs me when I leave Fremantle, begs me not to go, so many dead here in our country; horrible he says. And he knows these troubles first-hand. But Don, I am not sure he understands, and *si*, I have been on my own mission of course."

Even before leaving Melbourne, Michael had heard Peru could be dangerous, Clive talking of cancelling and only reassured by The Frenchman, then the Peruvian Interior Ministry at the last minute. The government was in control, and the troubles over they said, if visitors kept to the tourist routes, were not foolish, and did not wander. Maricielo's single eyebrow was raised.

"No Michael, these things cannot simply be erased and the world must know. So, how does this terror begin? The banks, they first nationalize, and the trouble begins with *Fascisto* government death squads. Many Michael, they go missing, twenty thousand dead. I see it myself, the buildings in the larger towns, the villages too, the fear, the damage, wrecked walls, and the slogans: paintings of machines are the mark of the *Fascisto* progress - the hammer and sickle for the *Comunista*, 'The Shining Path'. I hear of the torture, the intimidation in the countryside, the murder, the towns deserted, the stink of dead animals that hang from street poles, Michael, and the piled-up bodies, whole families dead, the local mayors murdered. So many bad things happen here, a giant copper mine that scars my country, my mountains, my people exploited."

"So Michael, do we simply forget these things? Can we forget? No! These things are so horrible that we cannot ever erase them from our souls. My father, he says like Spain, that in Peru the dead are more alive than the dead of any other country in the world. That is Frederico Lorca of course Michael, the great Spanish poet."

Michael recalls the tears in Maricielo's eyes and now understands how an experience like that could change a person. And now, with Don's notes, he sees the young writer taking chances, wandering the mountains in a tattered pair of sandals, many of his boxed-up stories like Grimm's Fairy Tales. Maricielo had paused while gathering her thoughts. "Ah, the stories. He writes to me, works at the mine, the first I see of this connection with your Aboriginal people. And I feel he is changing. But I also understand this Michael, the importance of the land, having the family roots, something that binds us."

Maricielo was leaning forward, Michael drunk but sober enough to feel uncomfortable, a tear down her cheek and a voice so low, bare arms and hands finally still. "At first, I am surprised at these feelings that grow, where they come from, thinking more of Don each day. I know this must be something special. Something very special. And now I listen to you here Michael, the talk of your family so far away, the two sweet children you have; and I think *si*, I am almost thirty and this something I want too."

"In the beginning, Don is at the mine, he answers my letters often, talks of the *Español* he is learning, because I say so. There is hope, and I think he may come. But it is many months since I see him, the absence and the heart that grows fond. I remember he is handsome and *si*, he is different. But I am here Michael, him so far away."

Michael lifts his head, yawns, and gazes into the office window. He rubs his eyes, but still sees the younger Maricielo back in Peru, hair falling across her face, cheeks wet, the painted lips smudged, and blowing strands of hair away from the corner of her mouth. He somehow smells the patchouli perfume and the stale cigarette smoke that hung in drifts from the vaulted bar ceiling in that lodge all those years ago. "So here I am Michael, alone, waiting. I write more letters while he travels in France, him a little lost I think, but most of my letters he does not get. And yet there is one letter I receive, finally with Don's promise that he will meet me. But he seems to disappear, before leaving France quickly. And my father, he worries, wants me back. I promise no more tantrums, no longer the ungrateful daughter who spat in his face. But I cannot come yet, Don not here. So, I am holding my breath."

Her eyes seemed to ignite. "And, so Michael, he arrives here, in my country finally. And yet, he is not quite here.

He hikes alone all the way from Cusco. Dangerous of course. I worry some will see him as a *Comunista* or part of some militia *Fascisto*. I worry he is shot or worse."

Michael understands the significance now, the danger, his desk loaded with stacks of Don's notes, stories of the young writer travelling alone, oblivious, ignorant or uncaring, the cards in a fine pressed metal box, his broken satchel bursting with hand-written notes.

• November 1990/Winay Wayna, Peru

I'm back at the tent, can't believe the news. Got some thinking to do, smoke a couple of spliffs, leave the flap open, shuffle Mama's cards & flick the top one over – A circle within a circle, a giant spoked wheel on the back of a floating man with a dog's head. On top of the wheel is a sphinx. There are clouds at every corner of the card, each with a winged beast of the zodiac & each reading from an open book.

I hear Mama's whisper weak, her favourite tortoiseshell combe broken, her face twisted & black hair a mess. Her white hand is soft on my shoulder, the lavender scent making me dizzy - Donatien, Donatien, but this is who you are.

But who am I? A scribbler all alone, my world just bits of paper.

Back at the bar I feel weird, push open the back door, Michael still here but Maricielo drunk like the old days, breathing heavy & head on chest. Don't feel like I'm anywhere, Mama gone, me floating & a long way from anywhere.

***

Michael knows now the name `Donatien' is French, but it feels so odd to see it written in Don's own hand. And Michael to this day does not recall where Don reappeared from, suddenly back in the bar and right there at the table. But it is no surprise to Michael that Don would imagine he could hear his mother's voice.

Maricielo had passed out in her chair, her empty glass smeared with lipstick and the lodge all quiet. There was smoke hanging from the ceiling and the low groan of a generator out back. Michael still cannot imagine what it would be like to receive news like that, so far from home and with his mother dead in tragic circumstances. And yet Don had said nothing at the time.

Michael shuffles more notes on his office desk and remembers staring at Maricielo, a handsome woman, head slumped forward and her breathing heavy. And then there was Don, his gold chain shining against a brown neck, wide-eyed and listening to every word. Michael did not get it back then. Why would his boozy childhood memories of the old Ebenezer Mission be of interest to anyone?

He shakes his head and brushes the greying curls away from his forehead, remembering the lodge barman with the wispy moustache, so keen to close up and get away. There was a soft woosh of wind in the mountains outside. Michael squints at his office desk. His drunken musings had forged a surprise connection back then; Don was impressed with

Michael learning some *Gunai* words in secret while the Ebenezer Aboriginal kids were forced to speak English in public. And now it makes more sense. Don was more comfortable with Michael from that point on, opening up right then and blurting out an unexpected apology. The young writer had recognized Michael from the cliff face after all, and Michael had forgotten to ring Jennifer.

| **26** |

Each day at the office blends into another. Now it is late afternoon, Michael at his desk, and the clang of another tram outside. He stares at Don's notes and continues to shuffle and sort: anything from Peru. He reads the heading and first few lines of the top page. He has a twitch in his right eye, distant memories from thirty years ago, leaving the lodge early for Machu Picchu, the last downhill leg through dense jungle, then the outer city walls. He recalls the sweat, the gloom close and engulfing, The Frenchman's breathing loud when they slowed to peer ahead. Paco, their guide, was upfront but stopped dead in his tracks, a torch beam way ahead, piercing the black but bouncing here and there. Michael rubs the back of his neck, the tingling again as he reads on.

• **November 1990/Machu Picchu, Peru**

With Mama dead, I need to get home. At least that's decided. Down from the lodge, my torch beam lost in cold night air, across the walls & through the city. Maricielo will be fine. But something stops me on this ridge. I catch my breath & light a spliff, this a sorry business, bodies wrapped, half wrapped & left, some new in white shrouds on beds of rock, flat & cold, jagged shadows that move with the moon.

Endless steps are worn & rounded from the passing of many feet. Here is a corridor, walls of rock both sides, wrought one side & living on the other. A scarlet fuchsia peers from a crack in the stone, the air thin but wet. Openings are windows, the dark and the gaping, clouds flashing, racing shadows, the valley, town & train below.

Stone walls are cold & black, the empty doorways blacker, barred & no one home. Here there's no bar, the owners inside but sick & failing, fearful whispers, wretched coughs & moaning, the smell of death, of fruit & cardamom. I peer between the houses, torchlight on mounds, on paths & steps. A single figure slumps, back to the wall, legs extended, head lolled to one side, still eyes staring, other bodies flat, some face down, the burial ground too small, the last priest waiting. He thinks this sickness is a call from the sun for those left to come & join him.

| 27 |

Don's notes continue to bring it all back for Michael: the wonders of Peru, the buildings real, impressive, and something tangible, all about structural design and artistry. And then there was Machu Picchu, the jewel in the crown, Michael pushing past vines to the outer fortifications, the drizzle-shrouded ruins. He sits at his desk and shakes his head at the thought of it: 1990 and Don on his way home after the death of his mother. He shuffles the notes on his desk and never could he have imagined that it was Don up ahead.

Michael still wonders at the impossible scale of the place after thirty years, the terraces massive beyond belief, the path a finely crafted knife edge ridge, not two people wide, ending with a towering peak high above it all. Empty stone buildings lined rock-hewn streets, a spider web of walkways connecting city squares and terraces. He remembers the walls were different, like nothing he had heard of, enormous blocks placed in the bottom row for extra strength in earthquakes, narrow stairs with tight twists and turns, unexpected corners, and dead ends. He had wondered what his builder father would have thought. More stairs fell from sight, often wedged between faces of rock, and stone balustrades were cut from a single ledge. Giant openings were windows, wider at the bottom than the top, also for added strength and each set in fine-cut stone. For Michael, it was structural perfection.

Way below, a bus travelled a switchback road from the gorge and village, then a railway connection through to Cusco, straddled by six thousand metre peaks. He remembers the swarthy complexion of Paco their guide, the Indian's talk of mountain spirits and horrendous rains while leading Michael and The Frenchman to a new tourist hotel in the shadow of the old main walls. "*Si*, it is true, *Señor* Michael, the spirits not happy with too many tourists, the rock and mud falling from up high, down the mountain, and on my people in the village. And yet we need the new buildings, and the government the money that tourists bring. For we are a poor people needing jobs, while keeping the mountain spirits happy with offerings and respect. So, you see, it is difficult. This balance we need."

Michael gazes up from his desk, thinking of the young writer wandering those mountains alone in dangerous times, sometimes in the dark and with very different priorities. He squints, preoccupied back then with the like of ten-tonne pieces of granite lifted to great heights and fixed in place with hand-hewn spigots. And it dawns on Michael, The Frenchman's latest email like a wakeup call, the darkest, pre-Eskimo imagery leaving an imprint on his impossibly tired brain, a prompt that possibly there may be other things at play here. Don's boxes had certainly re-ignited The Frenchman's interest and Michael's from almost thirty years ago. Michael smiles to himself, recalls those Frenchman lectures on archaeologists and an empty city where people worshipped the sun, cultivated five-hundred types of potato, and then just disappeared into thin air. He can see The Frenchman now, those heavy wire-rimmed glasses slipping low on his nose, with a new wife and time on his hands.

Michael still worries about falling down this rabbit hole of boxes, his desk full of the last of Don's Peru notes, and his memories of The Frenchman. "Never be fooled, my friend, by your so-called certainties. We are talking of civilization, *oui*, with a dash of something we call the human spirit or the soul, the roles of ritual, the shamans and priests, more than just heaven and earth."

| 28 |

Michael had waited with The Frenchman and Paco on the tourist hotel veranda, the tables and benches being otherwise empty. Morning sun arrived in brief bursts with any small talk drowned out by rain pounding on a flat tin roof and water gushing over the veranda gutter. He recalls the walls of Machu Picchu distorted and blurred, like his hungover thoughts of Don and Maricielo from the night before. Michael's eyes had finally focused on a lone figure emerging from the city walls, raging water knee-deep and the long Afghan jacket familiar.

Maricielo was suddenly on the steps in front of Michael, shivering, soaked, alone and bedraggled. The battle to cross had left her breathless; the heavy jacket was eventually discarded and dumped across the back of a bench, exposing the tiny black dress and lace-up boots. Her long hair clung to bare shoulders, mascara streaks like warpaint, and her lower lip aquiver. "All I know Michael, is that I had him, and now he is gone once more. I don't know if he tries to wake me in my tent, but he leaves a note in the dark, and I think this is really *adiós*. Me, I sleep late. *Si,* like the old days. The Night Manager, he asks me if Don is OK, but I am drunk still, so how do I know? *Si,* it is this Manager that tells me the bad news. The message to Don is from the Lima Consulate. Don's mother, she is killed in an accident."

Michael stares down at the notes on his desk, gazes across at the University through the elm street plantings, memories of Maricielo's wet clothes and patchouli, her dress hanging, wiping her eyes and nose, a stifled cough from bluish lips. After their late night, Michael wonders what he must have looked like, the hot and sticky air, the steam rising from the wet city ruins. His head throbbed. He had unbuttoned his vest and grabbed his jacket from the hotel railing, stepped out from the veranda, the searing sun ferocious.

He recalls a single white cloud clinging to the impossible pinnacle above the city ridge, shielding his eyes from the glare with one hand and turning to look back in the direction of the lodge. It was all about Don - like it is now - that night at the lodge above Machu Picchu, Don's empty bottles of sarsaparilla littering the table. One smoke followed another, Michael still astounded at Don keeping the bad news of his mother a secret, even from Maricielo.

Then there were the goodbyes, Maricielo folding her sopping Afghan jacket and drifting from the veranda to an almost empty bus, her hands and cheeks wet, hazel eyes down to the ground and her own lace-up boots.

Michael gazes about the office, Clive's desk and bookcase.

He cannot believe it is almost thirty years since that day, another time, another world, Maricielo climbing aboard that empty bus, her face pressed against the back window. There was a stifled wave, her black hair still wet and flat, Michael hungover and foolishly thinking this thing would end there and then.

| 29 |

Michael parks the car, walks into the empty house and flicks on the lights. He leaves his briefcase on the floor and drops on the couch. He stares at a framed photograph of his wife taken before the twins, her red hair shining. Jennifer is still in Cairns, probably another frangipani evening warm and clammy, the ceiling fans ticking over and the last of the sun through the palms outside. He hopes her father is under control, Jennifer, her sister and mother chatting on the veranda with their gin and tonics, but without the old man. Her mother would be asking after the kids, both grown up with their own lives, and Melissa with a big company bonus.

Jennifer is a talker and has been since University. She says Michael overthinks most things, with him the first to agree, these boxes making him mull over the most mundane questions. And Jennifer is clever; she knew something was bothering Michael when he returned from Peru. And now this thing is back, and he just never knows where to stop, with these late nights and headaches tangled up with Don's cards and these boxes of notes. She worried about leaving him alone in the big house, alone in the office too; Clive is rarely around these days.

Michael leans back into the couch and remembers coming home from Machu Picchu right on Christmas, walking in the door to a barrage of hugs and questions, the twins demanding to know all about the Indian kids: Did they drink Coke or Pepsi? Did they like ice cream? He can still see the smirk on young Christopher's face. Did they have to go to school?

He smiles to himself, always preferring the quiet life. There were plans for a family from the start, a brand-new housing estate with lots of space. And it was so good to be home for Christmas, Michael increasingly homesick in the months away. He sighs. Both the twins had short attention spans when kids, Christopher propped in front of the TV and flicking between channels, Melissa going from one doll to the next. The mandatory fight over Christmas presents needed a judgment call from Jennifer. He remembers his jetlag daze after the long flight home, a board game, a beer knocked over, and Jennifer sorting things out.

His mother's presents were always the last opened. They must be useful, she always said; something they need. She worried about the colour or the size of the gift and if Jennifer would approve. Michael ate too much every Christmas, ending up on the floor among mounds of torn wrapping paper.

And there was something about living on a corner, the twins making friends so easily, all the neighbours like family: Auntie Peg and Uncle Jeff next door, in the side street, no kids of their own, their gifts dropped off Christmas Eve. Then there were the real aunties and real uncles, including Jennifer's black sheep brother. She would never hear a word against him, and he was a favourite with the twins. She says they saw something in her brother that most do not see. Michael agrees he is a worker, good with his hands but drinks too much, the gruff and grumpy type, not a bit like Jennifer or the other sister. He was always in trouble with their father.

With the Christmas roast and dishes sorted, Jennifer would finally relax, sitting cross-legged on the floor, Michael with another beer, at ease in his leather rocker. His mother would fall asleep after a few pages from her latest Stephen King. With Jennifer's brother leaving, the twins would pile in the back seat of the Holden, drop off Michael's mother, and then it was the Christmas route march to Jennifer's school teacher sister.

But Michael's world has moved on since 1990, the twins have gone from the family home, and Jennifer's father is on the verge of dumping her black-sheep brother - again - this time once and for all, setting her father on a collision course with his wife and both daughters.

Michael sniffs and swears he can still smell the cat pee from Don's notes back in the office. He stretches his legs, kicking a cushion off the couch. Clive was right of course. "This Kiddo, never was finished with Don's funeral." Michael rubs his knee, raises himself on one elbow, looks at his running gear piled in a corner, and wonders if impact exercise is a good idea at his age. He had hoped it would clear his head and help him sort through loose ends that bother him like a reoccurring dream. But there is a wan smile as he thinks of Jennifer, twirling the now-grey hair behind her ear, a screwed-up nose, and even more freckles these days. She would always remind him of the obvious, long runs giving him too much time to dredge through every little thing: revisiting Peru and the accident, and the last time he was in this head space: her black sheep brother smashing up their father's car in 1997, her and the kids rushing to Queensland and Michael in West Australia for Don's funeral.

| 30 |

Don's funeral had worried Michael. At first, he had searched for excuses not to go. He was younger in 1997, inexperienced and uncomfortable with knowing no one other than Don's girlfriend, Maricielo. And that had been his first funeral since his own father's. Clive was busy, full-time back then, working on a shipping union study riddled with vicious wharf disputes. To make things worse, the funeral had been postponed at the very last minute due to a delay with the post-mortem.

If Michael thought he could escape the funeral due to limited available flights, that was soon ended by his old boss reminding Michael that he had Don's pressed metal card case after all, by mistake or design. He also had Don's gold neck chain. "Listen Kiddo, you'll regret it if you don't. I mean, you do know him. And did he not chase you down here, all the way from Fremantle?"

Michael can still see the Andy Warhol bouffant, the colour of straw back then, with the colonial lambchop sideburns, those ridiculous moleskin hi-pants one size too small, and that ratty tweed jacket he used to wear. He is conscious of the house being empty again and recalls the plane trip. He had adjusted his seat belt and shut his eyes, the newly inherited cards and fine gold chain a bulge in his vest pocket. Sleep did not come, and he had wondered about the days ahead and how Fremantle could have shaped the young writer. The plane arrived at the airport early, and Michael threw his overnight bag in the taxi boot, stepping into the passenger seat. He squinted, the driver with sleeves rolled up and hailing from one of the newer suburbs. "Freo? You're paying the bill, mate, but the place is still a dump, in my humble opinion, full of artsy types and do-gooder oddballs."

Michael was barely listening, his eyes tired and half-closed, the taxi racing; fleeting streetscapes blended to one until finally in Fremantle proper. He focussed on the actual buildings, some run-down but many renovated. He guessed the place had changed since Don was a teenager in the '70s and was suddenly aware of the driver. "Changes? Well, mate, I'll put you in the picture. It's all about The America's Cup, or was; sorting this place out a bit at least, and us beating the Yanks at their own game, ay? All that money spent in the lead-up to the 1987 defence, the whole place getting a bloody spruce up. Yeah, mate, it's now got some stuff for you tourists, ay: a couple of art galleries, some fancy cafes and restaurants to spend your reddies."

Closer to Maricielo's place, Michael's apprehension grew, wondering what had happened between her and Don: the young writer saying nothing in Melbourne at either of their two meetings. The driver had cursed, breaking Michael's train of thought, the taxi stopping at a dead-end lane. "It's these bloody roads mate! All dead ends and crazy angles." Michael peered out the passenger window to a round concrete bunker of a building that overlooked a small bay. He had paid the man, thrown open the door and made his escape.

Michael unfolded Maricielo's Street map on top of a wide concrete wall and gazed around to get his bearings. He squinted at Maricielo's map again, a maze of streets and lanes, then directly in at the bunker's large dome. "Funny," he had thought, an odd reminder of the synagogue near Don's accident. Michael's eyes followed his finger on the map: 'The Roundhouse - first permanent building in the Swan River Colony - 1830 to 1831'. He had frowned, picked up his overnight bag, and headed for Maricielo's place, only minutes away.

Out front of the warehouse, he stood on the road and looked up, the toes of his desert boots to the bluestone curb, a high single-storey facade with cream flakes of patchy paint peeling off a red brick wall. An older model Peugeot was parked out front, cobwebs draped from a cracked side mirror. He dropped his bag, turned his head, and gazed down the lane to the docks at the end, the giant rusted hull of a moored freighter high above the cobbles. Michael shook his head, picked up the bag, and stood for a moment more. He guessed the entrance was once a grand affair, a high flight of flagstone steps to a double door set in a heavy frame, now shuttered with grey-weathered boards.

He pulled a note from his jeans pocket to confirm the address, the numbers on the wall burnished brass, one loose and upside down. At street level, a small side gate seemed an afterthought, squeezed between the facade and the neighbour's brick wall. Above the gate was a single word on a wooden plaque: 'Yoga'. Michael remembers the painted letters, the ship's horn blaring, and the tingle on the back of his neck. He had leaned closer, the brush strokes similar to the note on the killer tree in Melbourne. Michael squirms at his desk just thinking of it: the now familiar upward and leftward lean of Don's writing.

He had unbolted the gate, narrow and makeshift, clambered over the low threshold, ducking his head and pushing his bag through the opening. The path was barely one-person wide once through the gate, with the brick walls on either side. He stepped over a low pile of rubble, boots crunching limestone toppings, a cloud of dust, broken brick dirt, and old wood: at the far end, an iron gate swung with a drawn-out craunch.

The square courtyard was small, and the patchouli incense a reminder of Peru and Maricielo. Brick walls rose from three sides, the central fountain a circle on a low square plinth, and the trickle of water through tiny clumps of flowers, electric blue and white. Michael forgot where he was for a moment, on the other side of the country for the funeral of a man killed in his prime. He now realises that was more like the beginning of the story, rather than the end.

The fountain water was calming, Michael just standing there, the flower reflections on a small black pond and the blue sky above a mottled mosaic diffused by green fern fronds that hung from a criss-cross of dark timber beams. Turning from the courtyard to a glassed-in living area, all seemed quiet, the warehouse a single-story lean-to structure. He fidgeted with the cards, shifted from one foot to the other, and stared at his reflection, then through the glass to sunbeam stripes on a bare timber floor. His eyes finally focussed on Maricielo's back. She was even smaller than he remembered, her plain black dress like a tiny tent and the club armchair way too big, raven-black hair, shorter, but still straight as a die.

To Michael, she looked lost in the corner of that big open room, his eyes drawn to a brown leg thrown over the arm of the chair and out to one side, open magazines strewn on the floor here and there. He hesitated at the thought of waking her, finally tapping on the glass. She tossed her hair from one shoulder to the other, straightened in the chair, and swung around, rising in slow motion and standing there, black dress just above the knee and mohair cardigan off one shoulder.

| 31 |

Michael had watched Maricielo approach the door in slow motion, pulling it open, white teeth against olive skin and hazel eyes welling with tears. He felt her bare arms tight around his neck. "Welcome, Michael. So good of you to come. Oh, and so sorry about the funeral being delayed." He dropped his overnight bag to the floor and stood back with thumbs in his vest pockets; Don's cards reminded him why he was there. He looked away, squinted, and pushed the bag aside with his foot.

He thought her smile forced, both consumed by the silence but drifting inside and away from the door. Maricielo suddenly stopped, seemed to take stock of things, turned, and waved back to where Michael had just walked in. "It is no good, Michael. I need to get out for a while; some fresh air, please. OK, if we walk? The morning sun is warm." He nodded, and they left. Nearer to the beach, her words burst out in fits and starts. "Ah, *si* Michael. There are so many changes

since Perú. Father is happy to have me back, of course, but..."
She shook her head.

Michael had no intention of pressuring Maricielo, and he would give her as much time as was needed. His thoughts wandered. It had been seven years since Peru and then those two fateful Melbourne meetings. He watched as Maricielo's hazel eyes fixed on The Roundhouse where Michael had escaped from the taxi driver. The walls were ridiculously thick, that odd concrete dome unnerving. "You know Michael; I still see him here every day; this his place." She sniffed, Michael offering his handkerchief. Again, he waited, and her eyes welled up.

"But how does such a thing happen?" Michael shook his head. There were rivers of tears, only stopping when she blew her nose and offered a stiff-lipped smile. "Such a crazy world. But Michael, you have not changed." More sniffs and a shrug. "Tomorrow, you shall meet Robbo." She turned away, her stare clouded, and out to sea. "But today, you will meet Angela, Don's sister." Her eyes had narrowed, and Michael detected a frown.

Back at the airport, Michael observed the two women, Maricielo's greeting cool, that raised eyebrow working over-time. Those two were not the best of friends, and Angela with a bad flight to cap things off. He guessed she had been drinking, probably with something else to help her through. He reminded her more than once that they had never met.

Michael remembers the suitcases and bags, a mountain of them, and a challenge to fit in the old Peugeot.

Michael is conscious of the empty house, his running gear still on the floor where he left it. He rubs his eyes and sits upright on the couch, distracted by a passing car outside the empty house and the thump of tyres over the speed hump. He wonders at the difference between siblings; Angela has such a strong presence in Don's notes, obviously close yet different. Michael nods to himself.

The Frenchman had lots to say about that in Peru: "Common ancestral backgrounds," he said, with copious theories on pronounced differences and the often-mysterious ways of brothers and sisters. Michael squints and rearranges the cushions at one end of the couch. He still sees The Frenchman's steel-grey eyes behind those thick glasses, pushing his psychology siblings barrow, his theories on acquired spiritual leanings and such.

The trip from the airport to Maricielo's warehouse was mostly silent. Michael was in the front passenger seat, with the occasional sideways glimpse in the rear-view at the bleached blonde in the back behind Maricielo. Don's sister was rakish with a smokey tan and Michael watched as she poked at her hair.

"Oh, I must look a freakin' treat, Michael." Michael

had noted the exaggerated sigh. "I always say there's no excuse for bad grooming."

Maricielo's eyes were slits whenever Angela spoke, her knuckles white and the gear stick bumping Michael's leg. She steered the Peugeot into the warehouse lane and bounced it up the bluestone kerb. He extracted the cases from the boot and back seat, Maricielo going ahead to open up. Michael grabbed Angela's arm as she hobbled and lurched across uneven flagstones to squeeze through the gate. Maricielo and Michael lugged the cases from the gate, down the side, to the courtyard, and inside to where Angela was waiting. "Does this dump have a bathroom?" Michael recalls the words more of a drawl.

Angela's cheeks were a red blush, her black lashes long. A heavy gold necklace hung from her neck. She looked dazed. "Understandable," thought Michael. But it seemed Maricielo had seen it all before and Angela disappeared to the front rooms.

Maricielo shuffled chairs to face the courtyard and dragged the cork from a bottle of red wine. Michael wondered how much she remembered from their first meeting. She sniffed. "Ah, Michael, I am still so embarrassed, accosting you in that lodge, me so drunk. What must you have thought about me?"

Michael was relieved she seemed to have forgotten how drunk he had been on that night in the lodge above Macchu Pichu. And he was keen to know what had happened between Don and her. "Well, we renovate this place after *Perú,* and he tells me a little of France, something that does not go to plan. He is disappointed at getting sick and not finding what he needs. Now, this is something I understand; being lost a little when in Fremantle, looking for the roots I mean. And he spoke to the neighbours back then." Michael watched as she peered into the bottom of her glass. "And he always listens, to everyone, maybe way too much." She smiled and reached over, Michael startled by her tugging his forearm. "*Si*, he listens, like you Michael."

"So, this is the first I truly remember of his stories here in Fremantle. There is a studio close to here that everyone, the locals they know. I learned that a man who owns it, or once did; he is an Italian artist, a sculptor. But this man is dead they say, for many years now. And I see this is odd." She tossed her hair from one shoulder to the other. "So, Don, of course, he is meeting this man, and they talk. Don tells me this sculptor is dressed in a grey smock and a red cravat. Every morning Don passes the studio, and this dead man waiting at the mailbox it seems. But to the new owner, Don is outside at the mailbox alone. The owner, he asks me what this is about; thinks it is a wind-up."

Maricielo shook her head. "In the beginning, Don and me, we share all these things, we talk, and I am thinking, these stories, such detail. He is a writer after all. And there are also the things I hear of his mother. So yes, I listen too. Next, he tells me of a room in a building, another place close by, this one owned by the University, with a Chinese man who lived and died there." Maricielo takes another gulp of wine. "What can I do? This is the way things become, and they are getting worse."

"He has his own worlds, but here we are in Fremantle. He does not drink, of course, but in one year, he is smoking many more joints, restless, like he is treading the water. He becomes compulsive and moves the furniture every day. A small thing. You know Michael, it will not stop. In the end, the stories are too much, and he comes and goes."

"In bed, I lay at night, his side empty, cold, pillows only. I hear the door, his steps, and the iron gate it grinds. This is late, night-time. He walks in darkness." Michael squinted, caught in the spotlight of Maricielo's teary stare.

"So, I am worried, of course. Is he sorry for the way things are? Why does this happen? So, I am thinking this is still about his mother, her so strange, everyone says. Her cards are with him always. But then I see something else, not so much his mother but now his father, and it is you, Michael, the things you say in *Perú*. He remembers them." Michael fumbled with the card case in his vest pocket, and she smiled for the first time.

"*Si* Michael, I remember too. Me so drunk. Here in Fremantle, he talks of the connection you have started. He reads all he can find, talks of the country, trails we cannot see, vibrations in the earth, bad things that stay, song lines, and snake spirits. But things, they get more *loco*."

"In the daytime, he lives in his writing." Maricielo tapped the arm of her chair. "Sits here, stares out to his garden, and I must think of my yoga, my clients, my income. There is talk, some not so comfortable, so I tell him, please sleep or go outside when I have the classes. So, I find him at The Roundhouse. He sits on the ground, his back against the wall of concrete."

Michael recalls Maricielo's empty glass on the floor, her elbow on the arm of the chair, and her chin on her fist. "And I am thinking the way things will go. Don, he still reads his mother's cards sometimes. There is the piles of paper, the mess everywhere I look." She frowned. "I say to Don again about my classes. My clients, they will leave. And we do not have the money for all this marijuana. Funny, I hear myself, sounding like my own mother."

She leaned over to reach the bottle, her cardigan loose and floppy. "My Don, he does not shave, no longer the boyish face, papers everywhere I turn. I hope for the sun to rise one morning and for the nightmare to end. But you know Michael, I just cannot help him any longer. And then I am alone." Michael had frowned and nodded. She waved one arm across the expanse of the room. "I suppose after France, and with his mother gone, Don is on a new journey."

Michael had stared outside at the courtyard fountain, the tinkle of water barely audible. He had an answer about that at least. "So, that was it. He simply up and left." Michael shuffled in his seat, startled by the loud squeak of polished leather. Maricielo followed his gaze out the window and she continued. "So, what do I do Michael? I ring Robbo of course, Don's best friend. There is no one else. He tells me Don is in Melbourne, and I know he meets you at the café."

"*Si*, you, Michael, have seen him more than me in recent years." Michael nodded, feeling a twinge of guilt for some reason, Don having chased him down in Melbourne, not once but twice.

"We are together here for two years only. And I am thinking about how he comes from France to meet me in *Perú*. But now I see it: he comes because I push him." Michael stared, Maricielo shaking as she tucked her sopping handkerchief deep in a mohair sleeve.

| 32 |

Michael is back in the office, happy to be out of the empty house, although still preoccupied with his pre-funeral visit and what he can now decipher from Don's backroom boxes. His memories are of fading light in a distant warehouse courtyard, Maricielo turning on a lamp and pushing a small table between their chairs. "So, Michael, you know of Don's father?" Michael nodded. He had read the note on the tree and now the 'yoga' sign, father and son, with identical writing.

"Well, we are not sure about some things, the cards from his mother and a gold chain from his father. He tells me the chain has not been found." Michael was suddenly acutely embarrassed, pulling the card case from his vest pocket and setting it down on the table. He had lifted the lid away, taking the cards in one hand and picking out Don's chain with the other. He remembers the loud sigh and Maricielo's eyes welling up. "Oh Michael, thank goodness you have it! Don's vermeil gold chain." Michael passed the chain to Maricielo and watched as she draped it between her fingers and thumb, then gathered it up in both hands.

Michael was surprised she appeared to have no interest in the cards. "The cards? *Si*, the case is quite beautiful, but these are his mother's really, very plain condition, and the symbol of the power she had in the early days. Something I agree with Angela on."

She eventually raised one hand. "Ah *si*, I almost forget too. There is something I have for you Michael." Her hair fell over one eye before she jumped up, an empty glass tipped on its side by her chair. Next, she was pulling at a kitchen drawer and fumbling with a handful of papers, scrunched up tight like it might escape and fly away at any moment.

"*Si*, for you, Michael," she had said, the hand still clenched. "From 1991, when I return from *Perú*. I miss his mother's funeral. But I offer to help with his things in the old house. Very strange for me, his room kept like he has never been away."

Maricielo peered back to Angela's room, all silent, Michael's eyes glued to Maricielo's clenched fist, the crumpled paper bunched up tight. "Oh, sorry Michael, some of Don's notes from when he was a kid." Her face was flushed. "I keep them. I feel guilty, but he has no need."

Michael stands at his desk and squints. He could never have guessed that a handful of Don's notes would grow into a life story packed in seven boxes and now in the office

backroom. He can still see a heartbroken Maricielo standing in her Fremantle warehouse before the funeral, and he
remembers the rest of her story.

"First, we moved from his mother's house to here,
Michael. Don has some money. My father, he helps, but is
not so happy. He tells me this place is not good for a proper
house, too small for a family he says. It needs much work. He
is still not so sure about Don, where things are going with
him and me." She waved her free hand. "As you see, it is only
the one big room here, the bathroom, and two smaller rooms
at the front."

She leaned closer, the patchouli oil intense, her voice
so soft he could hardly hear. "You know Michael, it is so
strange. I feel I know you well, the connection with Don, I
mean. He tells me he is lucky to meet you; destiny, he says,
but suddenly gone for good. So, I see it is your knowledge,
your books, and the connections he sees with his father's
people."

"Oh, and please, no mention to Angela of Don's
father." Michael was surprised back then. "*Si* Michael, they
are the same blood, and it is Don's father who organizes
the funeral." Maricielo shook her head and her mouth was
twisted. "But, Angela, she is so angry; she has not heard from
her father since being a little girl. It is like he does not exist
for her. And this Angela, she normally gets her way."

"So here I am, in the centre and getting the blame."
Maricielo's voice was a whisper. "I can tell you, Michael,

about his mother; there is this grip I always see, her and the cards. But him and his sister? That is something I do not understand."

Michael recalls the sadness in her eyes, Maricielo reminiscing. "But you know Michael, it is odd when Don and I, we first work at the café together here in Fremantle. I am no good an example of how to behave." Maricielo had shrugged her shoulders. "But I change from this selfish girl who sees no one else but me, and is ignoring him. Next, I am in *Perú*, buildings wrecked and bodies in the streets."

"Then suddenly I see Don again, this time different after so many of my letters. So Michael, we live here in this warehouse. Don is busy working with his hands, his father's tools, and our plan to make this place special. But my father is still doubting, although I know I am always in his heart. He sees something that maybe I miss. I see the boy that will grow, with some help from my father, a future with my yoga. But Don loses interest and cares nothing for money. Father frowns and shakes his head. He asks how will we live?"

"I change my Bikram classes for something less hard; the middle road to suit my students. These are a handful only, the housewives and occasional worker that passes through." Michael remembers gazing across polished timber boards; the area was large and open. "We plan it this way, the living-room kitchen that overlooks Don's courtyard. The furniture is not so much, so no problem for yoga. We push it against the side walls and kitchen bench. With the summer, there is the occasional class at the beach, down by The Roundhouse."

Michael had almost forgotten Don's childhood notes still trapped in Maricielo's grip. "Ah *si*, sorry Michael. It was strange for me, to read, his writing so personal. And I do not recognise myself, other than my love for the Spanish poet Frederico Lorca. But *si*, I am such a different person now." She finally passed the notes to Michael and drifted off to the bathroom.

The next day Michael is back at the office, his desk a mess, the bell of a Melbourne tram outside, and the screech of steel wheels in the grooves of the tracks. He runs his fingers through his greying curls and picks at one pile of notes smaller than the rest, the same notes reluctantly given to him by Maricielo before the funeral. Yes, the writing is the same as in the boxes, that odd upward slant already formed, just like his father's, the pages smudged and crumpled but smelling of patchouli rather than cat pee. The header is top left like in the boxes, but there is something different with these early notes: the letters 'DDA' are added to the end of each header.

| 33 |

My thoughts are loud thoughts. Mrs Graves says so, Gracie & me not focused, don't talk or contribute in the classroom, should try harder. About these stories, write them down she says, how I feel, my favourite places, favourite things.

It's called The Roundhouse, somewhere I can sit & think, like being by myself. From here I see the tops of cranes that reach the sky, ships at sea on secret journeys, at the beginning or the end. I see the beach, a brown dog with a ball, wet with wagging tail, mothers on chairs, bare legs brown, coloured umbrellas, swimming kids & dads.

Waves push a sand castle, walls broken, a silly kid that cries, nothing lasts forever. Seagulls float where they want, when they want. Do they know where they are going?

• **June 1980 / Freo / DDA**

I miss Dad & wondered if it was about Siss & me. & I wonder if Mama will leave too. She does leave sometimes, her art class once a week, me at the window scribbling until she comes back. Mrs Graves asks me if I'm unhappy, but I don't know why she asks. Yes, it feels good to write things down.

I sit at Mama's feet, with always the whispers. I lean closer, the lavender in her hair & shawl. The nights darker, Mama with art class stories, of a fireplace that crackles & spits but the room still cold, freezing faces, a light slap but no one there. Invisible hands, chilled fingers soft on the back of Mama's neck. I see a forest of upright easels that dance late at night, pottery wheels that stop & start, empty stools & benches, footsteps in south wing corridors, women in dresses that float on the outside courtyard.

But there's always you Siss, reminding me I read too much, believe too much. But you Siss, are just a kid.

• November 1983 / Freo / DDA

I don't like birthdays & today I'm 16. Mama's present is special she says, a family thing & she's acting all strange. She pulls away the wrapping & I'm curious. It's a small tin case with some cards that rattle around. She says it was her father's, a funny present for a kid. She makes a big deal of the cards, but they look pretty wrecked to me. Tips them on the bench. There's one on the floor, & she whispers – *Oui*, this card, it balances the wrongs of the past, the stories of our lives, this woman with a gold crown on her throne. In the right hand, she holds the raised sword, set of scales in the other. Remember Donatien, sometimes an injustice we allow, it cannot be forgotten.

***

Michael squints and flicks over the page, these earliest of Don's notes more significant now, after being stashed away in his sock drawer along with the letter and Don's cards for twenty-two years; finally reunited with Don's erratic collection of life musings stuffed in a gaggle of stinking boxes. Michael reads on.

***

I escape to The Roundhouse whenever I can, the thick walls wet. I read the books, a bakehouse somewhere, a courthouse & gaol. I see the shadows, heads of men huddled, no space to turn. They don't know what they've done. 6 rooms like cells, the courthouse & basement, the harbourmaster's office & a morgue. The smell makes me retch & shake. They've hanged a kid, here in the dark, his body dumped flat on a slab of stone.

• **December 1985 / Freo / DDA**

Siss is jealous, a new girl at the caf, South American, perfect English & loves poetry, pitch black hair never been cut, one eyebrow weird, often higher than the other. She's fiery, short, older & always in black like Mama, lots of friends in the city.

Siss is the bossy type, shakes her head from side to side, waves her finger in my face – I'm warning you Brother! That girl's a load of trouble, a high opinion of herself. Trust me, she's a problem. Even her freakin father disowns her.

I know Maricielo's father is a high flyer, a mine engineer & a friend of the chef. The delivery bloke's from Peru too, says life is dangerous there, no place for a girl like Maricielo, a little black cloud in a dress who wants to save the world. Each morning I get to work, hear the crunch of the gears, Maricielo's Kombi in the carpark. She's busy today, a demo downtown at Forrest Place, yesterday some workshop. Often, she doesn't make it in at all. They ask me, but how would I know?

She thinks I'm strange, everyone does, does nothing half-way, gets pissed, sells dope, a party animal, late nights & yoga the next day, the yin & yang she says. When she arrives everyone knows it, hits the kitchen like a storm, loud, black hair shining, half smoked rollies with purple lipstick, wide eyes & windmill arms.

Today she really is all over the place, off her head, on about home, something about floods. I don't get it, but listen – The waters Don, they must overflow to let the flood rage, the way of things to get change. We know this. *Si*, the waters, they will return to the riverbed when they are good & ready.

One Sunday session she's legless by lunchtime. I want to walk or catch a taxi, will even drive her clapped out Kombi. She shouts, those flying arms & tits, insists on driving, erupts when I question her. There's a heavy army coat over that little black dress, but it's so damn hot. The Kombi stinks, beer, sweat & patchouli oil. I feel sick, too much sars. She'll drive no matter what – Ah, relax Don. *Si*, have a joint.

She rummages in her jacket pocket, pulls out a butt, half smoked, soggy, purple stained, wants to know what turns me on, explodes at the drop of a hat. What's wrong with me? I dread the thought of her & Siss in the same room. We fly past the casino, mount a roundabout & hurtle on. She tosses her hair from side to side – This new casino Don, all about money, the skyscrapers' battle with the heavens that cover them. Me, I am on the side of those who have nothing. And those that are not allowed to enjoy the nothing they have.

I never know what she's on about, quoting some dead Spanish poet. & she's worse when she's drunk, just all over the place, lets go of the steering wheel, the Kombi a missile, lurching around a corner. She drives like the devil, rollie in the corner of her mouth, murders the gears. Finally, she pulls over, stops her shouting, takes a deep breath with eyes half closed, head on her chest & hair across her face. She's asleep at the wheel.

Another Sunday she's tired of her poetry readings & arty farty student friends, dragging me out & up to the weir. The carpark's full, Sunday drivers & families on picnics, Kombi dumped in the middle of the road. She says forget them, those arms all over the place, wild black hair – Ha Don, it is just you & me. Let's go, *pronto*, to hell with them.

We head off down the track, her stumbling ahead in gravel. I reach a fork then stop. I feel her eyes from somewhere behind me, next her hand's on my bum – Don, the way is here.

I gaze to the north, the sun hot on my face, sniff the water, sandals full of sand. I turn to Maricielo, eyes glowing hazel, laughing lips purple. She pulls off her tee, drops the black dress around her ankles, G-string tossed on the nearest bush – Let's go, it cannot be so cold.

Later it's dark in the back, the Kombi & us alone inside the carpark, trapped but not caring, the boom gate down & locked. I roll over on the damp mattress, asleep but not asleep, not sure what to make of all this, what to feel, her tits pressed against my back, her breath all beer & cigarettes, those fingers up and down my spine – To burn with desire & keep quiet about this, *si,* it is the greatest punishment we can bring on ourselves.

At work I'm like nothing happened, yesterday another story, her busy, another week gone & the dope costing me an arm & a leg. She leaves early, another demo downtown at Forrest Place & her making noise about doing a runner. I wonder what it would be like somewhere else. Her father is worried, her doing what she needs to do, flashing eyes & windmill arms – *Si*, to help our people of course! There is the open cut mine near home, far too big & does not belong. But we have a new president now, another JFK, a new dawn in our country.

Maricielo's father shakes his head, her his wife's daughter, but I don't know what he expects from me. He says Peru is dangerous & her not understanding, doesn't know when she has it good. She'll choose her own path regardless, just like her mother he says. It does get me thinking again, itchy feet & a big world. But Mama's shocked when I mention I might move out. Siss goes ballistic – You're pathetic Brother, need to grow up & stop smoking that stuff. It's not that tart is it?

But you're only 17 Siss. & no, it's nothing to do with Maricielo. She'll do whatever she wants.

• January 1986 / Freo / DDA

So, I've decided to go, things impermanent, the vacant buildings, narrow lanes I've known since a kid, every dogleg & dead end, every paver & kerb, the Roundhouse walls, multi storied ships, cities of sheep, the stink of shit & greasy wool, wafts of salt, summer sun, warm drifts of air down waterside alleys.

We stand chatting at the front gate, me & Robbo, him head & shoulders above me. He's got everything sorted & somewhere to go, a new job with good money. He's staring – D, you OK?

I'm fine, don't know why everyone asks. He doesn't get why I'd let Maricielo go & say nothing, but what can I say? How am I supposed to feel? There's the sex I suppose. Robbo shakes his head, fiddles with a ripped flannelette sleeve. But when it gets down to it, I'm more worried about Mama than me, Maricielo not in the picture. Robbo shuffles in his cowboy boots, that open shirt, a mess of red hair. He agrees I should move on, but reminds me again – You've got to be jokin D. Look, I'll give you the drum, that girl is bloody special!

| 34 |

Michael pushes the notes to the side of his desk and remembers Angela stumbling from her room, eyes half closed, the warehouse smelling of Maricielo's toast and patchouli. The outside courtyard was gloomy except for a dull golden spotlight forgotten and left on overnight. Michael regretted the extra wine from the night before, a repeat of their first meeting in the lodge above Machu Picchu all those years ago. Only this time sleeping where they sat in the warehouse living room. His neck was stiff, and coffee mugs sat on the kitchen bench by Maricielo's still made-up sofa bed. He pushed a third chair between his and hers, trying not to stare at Angela's face, streaks of black under bleary smudged eyes and red lipstick. "Now I'm alone in the world, Michael, Brother gone and no family at all."

Everything was new for Michael back then, but now he knows more; Don's writing is peppered with mentions of his sister, younger but seeming so sure of herself. He recalls Maricielo's sideways glance, shifting from Angela to the outside courtyard and then back again. It was mid-morning, and they had resumed drinking. She asked to smoke without waiting for an answer, lifting her glass, gulping, and raising it to eye level as if inspecting it for dirt or imperfection. Maricielo sighed, and Michael was about to get the full story whether he wanted it or not. A cluster of rings crowded both hands, and a gold bracelet rattled when she spoke.

"To be honest, Michael, I got no help from anyone to get where I am; Mother with her own issues, thinking of herself and Brother most of the time." There were early jobs, but none that lived up to Angela's expectations. "Took a while Michael, me eventually getting noticed, my current outfit born in the mid-eighties and really going places; specialists in insurance and superannuation. Investment markets can be volatile," she croaked. "Wise to check in weekly with clients, put in the hard yards, monitor their investments and keep on top of things."

Michael had nodded in the right places, tricky with Maricielo in the corner of his eye and often shaking her head. Angela ploughed on. "Older companies are the establishment, no freakin' vision and going nowhere, review investments over too big a timeframe, more focussed on their historical investment cycles." Michael had lost interest in Angela's CV by then, staring out at the fountain, the dull spotlight still on, the shifting shadows on the courtyard floor. But something drew his eyes back to this woman, Don's sister, fumbling with her handkerchief, bracelet banging on the bottle as she poured another drink. He remembers the coughs and the determination to keep talking at all costs, her career a safe subject. "Mine's a smallish outfit, boutique-style. That's where the freakin' money is. We offer the personal touch and a full-on service to the corporate world with financial advice to a diversified client base on the Australian west and east coasts."

Michael shakes his head and recalls everything being too rehearsed, out to convince herself rather than him, especially with her brother just killed in a shocking accident. But there Michael was: staring again. He remembers Angela dragging a tissue from her sequinned jacket pocket, fumbling with a pack of Benson and Hedges, sniffing and dabbing her nose, those red eyes bleary and raised to the ceiling. Michael remembers her fingers tugging at her necklace with painted nails so red. A lone tear ran down her cheek and onto the front of her jacket. Michael was surprised at what came next. "I'm getting married, would you believe it? In the middle of sorting things in California and expecting Brother over for the wedding."

Angela had stopped, her eyes dropping to the floor. "Funny. It seems like yesterday, me just getting to know Brother when he suddenly left Freo and was off to that mine. There was Mother of course, but I suppose I was lonely. And there was Jackson. He was tall with wide shoulders and an American accent. And there were the sharp clothes, the double-breasted suits, and pleated pants. He was a fair-haired Adonis, just visiting back then".

Michael had wondered if she had heard that same Greek God was destined to spend half his life in the underworld. But Angela was not finished. "Mother never liked him, and he was certainly no Don. I don't think she cared when I moved out. But she sure did miss Brother. Jackson popped the question with some flowers and a bottle of Bollie; the plan for me to join him in California."

"He's a financier Michael, a good freakin' catch. So everyone says. Based in Perth for a spell and was a partner in his own business at only twenty-one. A college football star to boot. There'd been interest in opening a Perth office, the long-term economic forecast promising. So yeah, Michael, we'll marry in The States. I've already agreed to learn some yoga and have had a go at meditation." She stopped dead, a rare quiet spell, and stared at Michael. "He's sort of religious."

Michael shuffles more notes on his office desk and squints at the thought of what she had said. "She thought she could change him." By now Michael is certain that Don was no fan of religion, not the conventional type anyway. But there is something in his writing, something with Don and his mother. There are odd bits and pieces that float in and out of his notes, following Michael around like the smell of Don's backroom boxes.

He shakes his head, in his late thirties back then, knowing nothing of Don's prolific writing or his eccentric mother and still trying to work Clive out. He remembers feeling the intensity of Maricielo's stare but not daring to take his eyes off Angela. Don's sister seemed oblivious and continued her own story. "Jackson says every new member must improve their knowledge and embrace a vision of world colonies, including centres in the US and Europe, his family big into cremation." She lit another cigarette, Michael now wondering if this Angela was the same pragmatic and judgemental sister mentioned throughout Don's notes. "Yeah, sounds a bit heavy; I know Michael, human happiness needs spiritual awareness and all that stuff."

Michael was more than a little bemused, Angela with her gold necklace and bracelet, the sequinned blouse, Jackson the suited Adonis and the cultish religion of his. Michael could hardly hear, the words dropping off as if Angela was talking to herself, reaching for another tissue.

"Oh well, I'll make it work." She dropped her glass to the floor by the half-empty bottle, Michael thinking the glass might break. He remembers his head spinning; too much info too quickly. But there were so many loose ends back then, him gazing out to the courtyard, then back at Angela. What about their mother?

Angela took a deep breath. "Well Michael, I'm not sure what to say. Mother was not like other mothers. An artist friend once told her she had a 'gift' as if she needed any encouragement with that one. We were just kids, and I'd no idea what this 'gift' actually meant. Strange? Yeah, I suppose I caught on at some stage. But what I did know was that there was something between those two, her and Brother. I mean,

Mother was the only one who used his proper full-blown name: 'Donatien'."

Michael recalls catching his breath. That name, so odd to his Anglo ears, and Angela with another thin-lipped smile. "Yeah, I know, a freakin' mouthful. Bet she had no idea the grief it caused him. And that's what the teachers called him too; made things worse with his stories and stuff. Don really was fed up explaining where the hell the weird freakin' name came from; left it behind as soon as he could."

"Mother, she was something." Angela sighed. "But I do blame her for a lot of this stuff. I mean, Don thinks he can see things, talks to himself, has 'loud thoughts', and all that mumbo jumbo. No surprise there, considering what she filled his freakin' head with. I'm younger, but he's always been more like a little brother. Take everything he says with a grain of salt, and I say the same with Mother's stories. Funny, I get so peed off as years come and go." She laughed. "He knows I had no time for their freakin' fairy tales."

"I can tell you, Michael, it was bad enough for me, with a crazy French mother and the vegetarian thing. But for Brother, are you kidding? Donatien de Alain, here in Freo, way back then? No freakin' way!"

| 35 |

Michael stands at his desk and stretches his legs. He now sees the irony of that pre-funeral discussion over twenty years ago, Angela's life choice to sign up with some West Coast American cult but the whole thing lacking conviction. He scratches the side of his head and still wonders how that turned out. But he was more interested in Don's mother back then, and Angela was happy to fill in any gaps. "Me? Well Michael, I'd no chance with Mother being Mother. To be honest, I was embarrassed, her all over Brother from when we were kids, smothering him like, and her so erratic, especially when she drank. Who knows? Maybe that's why Brother never touched a drop of booze."

"She was French I suppose; the real thing, spoke it all the time, mostly to herself but sometimes to Brother. Even he couldn't see the freakin' point. Neither of us were interested, to be honest. And that sort of thing, well, it just didn't cut the mustard around here in those days. In the end, Mother's off the rails, Brother and me both gone, her having a tough time, not sleeping, crazy dreams, she said. Next thing, she's dead, some old fart in a pork pie hat and a brand-new Corolla. Gets his freakin' foot stuck in the accelerator pedal and runs up on the footpath."

Michael had sat there, shuffling in his chair, Don not mentioning his mother's death in either Melbourne meeting. "Yeah, Brother and I argued, but I worry about him heaps, so close to Mother, too freakin' close; those stories so weird and him always looking for something, a soft target, you might say. He reads all this alternative science rubbish, magazines, and oddball books, then goes off on a tangent with Aboriginal stuff. A real greenie in the end. Spent all his wages. But then, he never did care about money."

"Yeah, broke Mother's heart, and it all began with that Peruvian tart." Angela had screwed up her eyes, and Michael thought it all a bit much. But then he wondered if she was about to burst into tears, blowing her nose, cigarette ash in her empty wine glass, and a scowl in Maricielo's direction on the other side of the room. "Suddenly, that one, she ups and leaves Freo for South America. And Brother, he's off on a wild goose chase of his own."

Michael remembers Maricielo, sitting there quietly, cross-legged and flicking magazine pages, black dress, and bare feet on her sofa. She had eventually disappeared to the bathroom at the front of the warehouse; Michael left waiting for Angela's next blast, empty glass in one hand, scarlet-stained cigarette in the other. "Yeah, Mother was beside herself when Brother shot through. She kept all his stuff in a locked room like a shrine or something, his writing desk and stacks of books just the same. Oh, and there were his two cats as well, a shaggin' wagon wreck called Gracie that he dumped in Mother's garage. Almost nineteen when he left, me gone soon after."

"They were close Michael, but who does Brother ring when he's in trouble? Little old me. And it always has been. I just wish he could have settled down, for God's sake. After Peru and Mother's death, he didn't hang around for long; he moved to this dump as soon as that woman turned up again, his junk heap of a shaggin' wagon rusting away in Mother's garage, me dropping in to check up on the old place and feed his freakin' cats every single day. He never planned a thing in his life, no sense, care, or responsibility. I told him straight off: we should sell the freakin' house there and then. Yeah, I had a life to get on with too."

Michael can still see her sniffling, the handful of tissues, and then a scramble for matches. And yes, he can still see Don under Angela's makeup, the occasional uncertainty in those same brown eyes. "Funny the things you remember Michael. As a teenager, the girls were always keen on Brother. I see it then and knew it from my friends. They loved the suntan, that gold chain he always wore, the face of an angel, but so distant it was painful. Just couldn't freakin' relate. I think they just gave up in the end."

At his office desk, Michael squints and fiddles with the cards in his pocket. He thinks of the odd bond between those two and that long chat before the funeral, Angela slipping into occasional laughter, so unlike her brother. He had stared at Angela leaning back in her chair, the red lips, the unlit cigarette frozen between finger and thumb, the nails splashed with red, the clink of her gold bracelet. "And then Michael, there was the one about Mother and those freakin' cats. One day she ran poor Chloe over when backing out of the driveway without looking; she should never have been driving. She was away with the fairies at the best of times, knocked over the brick fence. Anyway, the poor little beastie had her legs and tail busted, a Vet bill of over a thousand."

Angela had stopped dead, sat there, lit a new cigarette, coughed, and gazed down at the wooden warehouse floor. For Michael, the whole thing is flashing back, sitting with Angela before the funeral over twenty years ago, more stories waiting in Don's boxes. "That vet bill Michael, well, it was a bucket of freakin' money in those days. To be honest, I would've put poor Chloe down. But Mother knew Don would never agree. He had a real thing about animals. But, look, Michael, I never understood either of them, not really. Suppose I was never part of that, whatever the hell it was."

"I remember one Saturday, he's back for a visit from the mine for Mother's birthday. They're at a magic fair of sorts, down at Freo market from memory. So, Brother drags her along before leaving for France to 'find his roots' or something. Funny, having those crazy cards since he was

sixteen but refusing to have his or Mother's fortune read."
Angela seemed to drift again.

"To be honest, Brother underestimated his impact
on people around him, could never read others, nor them
him. In his own bubble, that one." Michael had thought her
well drunk by then, the croak worse, brandishing the unlit
cigarette, the upturned ashtray on Maricielo's polished floor,
the slurred words, and spilled wine. But he had no reason to
doubt her, unlike Don's writing, where Michael has no idea
what is true and what is not.

"Yeah, quite the imagination Michael, but I can tell
you one thing for sure: Brother does nothing the easy way.
Insists on wearing those stupid freakin' sandals. Reads things
into stuff that just isn't there, preoccupied with France until
he's been there, then drops it like a hot brick - wasting his
time, of course. But still, he's always searching. Yeah, it all
comes down to Mother in my book. And that's where this
whole freakin' thing starts and ends. But she was brave; I'll
give her that, a big thing to emigrate out here. By herself too.
Especially after her own parents were both killed in some
freakin' boating accident she refused to talk about."

Michael sighs and stares at a stationary tram through
the office window, an irate commuter in a black beanie
remonstrating with the driver through the open door. But
he is thinking of Don, his mother and sister, the crazy family
stories, the coincidence, and now the boxes; the whole thing
on hold for twenty-two years and the memories of Angela

flooding back. "Well, after Brother left, something changed Michael. I noticed it: the greenie thing and all that. Stuff still bothers him, like it always freakin' has. Then there was France. What a disaster! I mean, he got sick, didn't he, real freakin' sick. Thank goodness for the Aussie Consulate. I can tell you, Michael; he sounded like shit on the phone, definitely not with it. Couldn't even eat. He sure as hell never ate much to start with."

"The doctors? They said it was a serious allergic reaction of some freakin' sort, made worse by not taking care of himself. He'd gone south, apparently. Had to get out of there quick smart; a problem in his guts, bad food, an odd allergy, or something..."

Michael recalls Angela stopping right there like she was waiting for him to say something or she was still mulling the whole thing over herself. "Like I told you, Michael: we're talking Brother here, but I believe him this time. He said the doctors really had no clue and thought it was all in his freakin' head. Well, God knows everything else is. Anyway, I tell him to get his arse back home, pick up your freakin' cats and sort out that wreck in Mother's garage. We don't need this grief. Rent a place of your own if you must, but not too far away. Next thing I know, he's bailed out, swapped France for Peru, in South freakin' America. With her."

| 36 |

Michael recalls being distracted by the clatter of Maricielo in the warehouse bathroom, the funeral the next day, and Angela drifting back to her room to rummage in that mountain of luggage. He browsed through lifestyle magazines until noticing a movement outside. There was a man in the courtyard with a daypack at his feet.

Robbo was Don's best friend, his back to the glass door like he was assessing Don's courtyard. There was the slightest raising of shoulders before picking up his pack, opening the door and staring straight through Michael until his eyes seemed to focus; Robbo was built like a beanpole, another redhead, and the same age as Don. Michael remembers the beery breath, the beginning of a beard and a faded blue singlet under an open shirt of frayed flannelette that hung outside his jeans. No neat casual happening there. He seemed to know his way around but dragged his feet, cowboy work boots with scuffed chisel toes.

Robbo headed straight for the fridge and fumbled with a beer, the clatter of a bottle top loud on the timber floor. He dropped on the nearest chair and took a swig from his stubby. The words came slow, Michael patient as always, the gaps long and disconcerting like he was thinking aloud. "Funny I reckon Mike... both you and me livin' in Melbourne, while D, he came and went – all over the place once he left Freo."

"It was me that left Freo first though, headed north, followed the coast to where the money was. North West Shelf mostly. He took my advice, I think. Had been nowhere until then, and I reckon somethin' changed."

"In the end, I got tired of the long hours up there, day after day, the driving and chopper flights offshore... and just bein' lonely, really. Never bothered him though."

"No one was more surprised than me when D turned up in Melbourne... been around the world by then, his mum was dead, and then the split with Maricielo... wouldn't tell me for months. But he mentioned you Mike, often; meeting you at some café, your books he borrowed... and all he needed on the Victorian Goldfields... a real bee in his bonnet about that one. I didn't get what he was up to, but..." His gaze wandered out to the courtyard. "Ya know what, Mike? He loved this garden. I do chat with Maricielo, but I'd forgotten just how beautiful this place is."

"I guess you won't know this Mike, but D and me, well, we shared a house for a while when he first came over to Melbourne, south of the river, just him and me. Getting his head together, I 'spose. But we go back a long way, lots of water under that bridge. Don't get around that much these days though, a family man like you... bank mortgage, wife and kids, the whole box and dice. Anne's mindin' the kids right now."

"Funny Mike, I met Anne in Melbourne through D; still can't believe it. At the beach... just south of the city, about

'93, I reckon." Robbo smiled. "It was D she took a shine to at the beginning." He shook his head. "He had no bloody idea... never did. I see the girls staring when he walks past all the time. Me? Was never in the frame. Even I couldn't read him, not really."

Michael recalls feeling even more uncomfortable at all that personal information, Robbo suddenly picking up his stubby and drifting outside, his boots a shuffle on the wooden floor. Angela and Maricielo returned. He had watched Robbo pacing the courtyard outside, back and forth, Maricielo brushing through the door and Robbo meeting her halfway outside. Michael knew he was again staring, Maricielo on her toes, brown arms barely reaching Robbo's neck, raven mane down the centre of her back, black dress hitched up, shoulders shaking. Robbo's face changed from grey to red, lips barely moving, and eyes screwed up.

Once out in the courtyard himself, Michael stood for a moment, unbuttoned his vest, Paisley shirt sleeves rolled up to the elbows. He sniffed the air, a hint of patchouli, the tinkle of water, and the flicker of shadows from ferns overhead. Michael watched Robbo, arm around Maricielo, on one of two garden benches. He wandered over and sat at the end. All three stared at Angela inside, Maricielo the first to break the silence.

"You know Michael; that one, she really is from another planet. Nothing like her brother. *Si*, Don is mixed up, but never a cross word about anyone. This terrible thing happens, and I know she is somehow blaming me." She turned to Robbo. "But it is this man I feel for."

Michael sits in the office, still uneasy after all those years at the thought of seeing Don on the very last day of his life. But that was nothing compared to Robbo's admission on that day before the funeral. "Yep, Mike... he told me, said you'd caught up outside the Theosophical Society. But I feel like shit... well, you know... guilty that I could have somehow changed the way things went."

Michael had turned to the door, a click from the latch as Angela drifted outside and stood by the fountain inspecting her fingernails, Robbo coughing and Maricielo clutching his hand. "You know," she whispered, "this is enough, Robbo! You are certainly not to blame." Her face was flushed, Robbo passing her a handkerchief and Michael looking away, straight through Angela to the bricks in the boundary wall, some fired orange-red, some with bits of blue, the smoke in a spiral from Angela's latest cigarette. Her hand moved, the jangle from her gold bracelet, the cigarette flashing red; on then off.

Michael's eyes dropped to the pond at Angela's feet, her stiletto shoes, one half-off and on its side. He had stared as she stubbed the butt on the fountain's edge, came over, and sat facing them on the second bench. Robbo's face was now white, and Michael thought he may be ill.

By now, it is late, and the office is in semi-darkness. Michael peers out the window, the University gate visible through the street elms, the first of the lights, his head full of the weeping wound of a killer tree, the hand-written note and the wet sap on his fingers, then the words of Don's father.

Michael squints; Robbo was a mess back then at the

warehouse. "Yep… I really felt for his old man. It was hellish Mike, hearing about that bloody tree, the accident. Someone from the bakery… they rang me at work the next day. And I'm still pissed from being out with D the night before, the same bloody night he was killed."

"He hadn't turned up for his shift. To top things off, it was my idea to meet with a couple of work friends that night. Shit, he never even wanted to be there, for Christ's sake." Robbo clenched both his hands and looked up. "They all liked him at the bakery but couldn't work him out, of course…. no trouble holding down a job whenever he wanted one… the patience of a saint, but no good with crowds or occasions. And who knows," he added, tugging at a ripped shirt cuff, "if we had gone somewhere else… well…?"

Michael had totally understood, Robbo reliving the whole thing in his head. And Michael still gets it, delving through Don's boxes; the question of the tree, the traffic lights, and the timing of the accident.

"The others drove," Robbo had continued. "Me, I would have hopped on a tram. No good to D, of course… that man a walking machine. Has to march everywhere in those bloody sandals of his." He lifted his eyebrows and shrugged. "So, guess what? We walk the whole bloody way… a couple of kilometres I reckon, first the pub, then a pizza next door."

"So… later… there's just him and me in the upstairs bathroom. I can still see him. He's standing at a small square window over the washbasin, the smell of pizza, a late tram passing outside. D, he's talkative… weird for him. Stone cold sober of course, on about his house up the bush, the rustles in the night, winters with gum leaves frozen like chandeliers, his precious mountain view, the moonlit nights..."

Robbo had stopped and turned to Michael. His eyes were half closed, stubby clenched tight. "Mmmm... just thought of it Mike, no booze of course, but not one choof that night. Yep, had completely given the dope away. Tired for sure, but sort of focused for him. In the end, we were back in the pub... at the bar, me totally skint and pissed as a newt. D emptied his pockets... never did give a shit about money, coins falling to the floor and rolling against the base of the bar with a bang. I bought one last round, and he went for a piss... 'all that sars,' he said."

"He never came back, Mike... left me and his bloody drink in that dive of a bar." Robbo blew his nose. "Another of his famous Houdini acts. He just shot through, out the back door, to walk all the way back to The Albert. Shit... never said a bloody thing." Robbo fell silent, Maricielo in tears, and Angela ashen-faced, Michael sharing Robbo's feelings of guilt but glad it was Robbo and not him at the very end.

Michael remembers staring out at the courtyard later, the fridge door opening, and Robbo with another beer. Maricielo grasped a giant coffee mug in both hands, and Angela looked up from freshly-painted nails. "God freakin' knows Michael, I never expected it would come to this. No one does, I suppose. And one thing for sure, Mother, she would never have coped."

Robbo agreed. "You know... I first met her as a kid, D's mum I mean. Don't mind sayin', I was scared of her at first. All in black, for as long as I remember. Oh, and black lipstick." He nodded to Angela. "I knew the other parents had no time for the poor woman. I heard it all, the gossip about the religious nutter, that witch down the street." Robbo's eyes were on Angela again. "But she had the kids to bring up and sure as hell doted on D... embarrassed about that he was."

"You need to remember Mike... about someone like her... Freo was different in them days... no cappuccino strip. D's mum was a veggo, too, pretty damn strict, probably where D picked it up. Those two were peas in a pod when he was younger... this bloody close." He held his right hand up and crossed his fingers. "And... that veggo thing, D would bot a beef sandwich at school when he could, and not opposed to the occasional pie and sauce. I reckon the kids copped some stick in them days. Reckon it toughened up Angie though."

Michael gave no thought to the boxes back then. He had the cards and a handful of Don's early notes from Maricielo. He could never have imagined inheriting these boxes over twenty years later, more stories, more questions. Michael squints at his desk and for a moment is reminded of Pandora's Box, another of his Greek stories, the box best left untouched. But no, Michael has come this far.

Robbo had just kept on talking on that day before the funeral. "We know the police went to D's room at The Albert Hotel. To collect his things. Yep... he had his hotel key on him. And he had your address in his pocket Mike, but not much else... always travelled light. He never carried a wallet. The police, they sifted through his hotel room, a bakery pay-slip on the floor... shoved his stuff in a milk crate."

"Never found his gold chain Mike, fine like a piece of string... never took it off as far as I know." Michael looked across at Maricielo, and Robbo paused while she explained.

"Mmmm. That's odd. Anyways, good that you had it, those cards to I s'pose. They did find that ratty leather satchel he always carried around for years, busted zip and all... stuffed full of his latest offerings, the rest left in his house up the bush... or stuffed in boxes in the corner of my bloody garage."

Michael remembers Angela on the phone for over an hour, a cloud of cigarette smoke, a wedding to organise, and Jackson back in California. There were also Don's cats to collect. Maricielo took two sleeping pills and lay on her sofa under an Andean woven blanket, Robbo slumped in a chair and Michael in the other front room, drenched in sweat and harassed by dreams, a tree that bled, The Frenchman's nightmare pre-Eskimo photographs, Don's cards and impending funeral.

| 37 |

On the morning of the funeral, Michael recalls an agitated Angela, haunted by a father who left in the early days. Her face was red. "Why would I not be pissed off? That worm crawling out of the freakin' woodwork, him and his gaggle of church-going cronies." Michael had no idea what was coming but did wonder if the church funeral was appropriate, even more now, over twenty years later and after reading Don's notes. He recalls Robbo standing, stretching to his full height, and taking a deep breath. "Well Mike, I've no idea... never really spoke about that stuff... I mean... his dad's Protestant but his mum's Catholic. Well, I used to think so... although, to be honest, I don't know if anyone had a clue what she was. Damn sure of one thing, though, D would never have wanted a church funeral of any bloody sort. But he never left any instructions that I know of. Crazy now I think of it... all that writing and no will!" Robbo fiddled with his shirt buttons, unsettling Michael with his blank stare until turning to Angela.

She shrugged. "Don't ask me; I doubt he expected to up and freakin' die. But I'm not fussed about this 'burial' stuff myself; Jackson is all for cremation, and real estate is expensive. Funny, Mother could never deal with the thought of it; burning the body, I mean. Had a thing about it and went ballistic if it was ever mentioned. Like Robbo says, you'd never know with Brother."

"Anyway, our freakin' father, that selfish little shit should never have been in the equation. How the hell could he have known anything about us? It was him that walked out, remember? His own freakin' family. I bet that after organizing this circus, he won't even have the guts to turn up."

Michael runs a hand along the lip of his office desk, lifts his finger to eye level, and inspects the dust. He remembers Robbo suggesting they meet Angela and Maricielo at the church. Robbo was keen to see Don's family house for old times' sake and insisted that Michael tag along. Michael nodded, always after the complete story.

The taxi stopped at a modest brick veneer with a 'To Let' sign out front, the grass overgrown and brown, the wire gate ajar, one gate pillar damaged, and three bricks from the top course laying broken against the fence. "Brings back memories, Mike... never fixed from when she ran over D's bloody cat and cleaned up the gateway pillar." Michael stood waiting, watched Robbo chat to the driver, then fling open the door and throw his long legs out and onto the driveway, his boots landing on the cracked concrete. He pushed on past; Michael paused by a waste high window sill, picking paint flakes from dry and cracked wood. Michael turned to follow Robbo through a half-open side gate to the backyard, Don's best friend standing still and staring at a rusted playground slide and swing.

"Angie was always teasing him as a kid Mike... about making up stuff. The earliest story I remember was of black men with beards down at The Roundhouse on the beach. Angie would run home to tell their mother... D being silly again." There was a blank look on Robbo's face, his mind obviously wandering, staring into the crooked back fence, the parched timber palings askew here and there. "You know what, Mike? D clung to that bloody story right through school. Old Mrs Graves sent him home more times than I can count for making stuff up. His mother never said a thing about any of that. Well... I mean, how could she? No bloody way, not with her and her own stories. But who would have thought back then that it was all true?

Michael had watched as Robbo floated around the backyard. "There was the time I put a steel garden rake through his bare left foot, us building castles, catapults, walls... oh, and moats... down there at the back. Hasn't changed a bit... more like a dust bowl than a bloody backyard. Perfect for Medieval sieges and battles though. No shortage of storylines with Don about. Anyway, the bloody foot got infected, and he ended up in hospital... couldn't kick a footy for months."

To Michael, it seemed like the two of them had just stood there in the yard for an impossibly long time, the driver finally sounding his horn out front. He remembers grabbing Robbo's limp left arm, leading him back to the taxi in silence, worried about what was coming next – the funeral of a man still in his twenties, killed in a freakish accident. Michael squints, fumbles, and rests Don's cards on his office desk.

| **38** |

At the Fremantle church, Michael had zipped up his jacket and stood in the courtyard alone while small groups drifted and settled in pockets. He stepped back, taking in the walls and surrounding roofs, comfortable with his known knowns of history, building, and architecture. The church was impressive, 19th Century, a mix of early English and Gothic, and a monument to early pioneers: a tough lot, intent on rebuilding their Old World right here in Fremantle, The Frenchman's words an echo in Michael's ears: "Not so much of the bricks and mortar my friend."

Inside he had peered around for a moment, the tiny congregation seeming overwhelmed by the volume of the place. The high-pitched ceiling was vaulted, nicely arched jarrah probably, impressive stained glass behind the altar and a brass lectern in the shape of an eagle. On the walls was an array of rectangular plaques, prominent past citizens and survivors of shipwrecks. Settling in the back row, he turned and scanned the faces of the last stragglers drifting through the door. Most were blank. Some wore frowns, and others with eyes down to the floor. He tried to imagine Don's father, what he would look like, not one face looking remotely like the young writer. That blonde up front was Angela. That beanpole was Robbo: Don's best friend, head and shoulders above the rest. To Michael, the clergyman's intro was not connecting, and he doubted the man even knew Don. A work colleague looked grim. His words wandered, mostly stifled and difficult, Michael's eyes lifting way above the altar, the morning sun shining through stained glass and igniting the words in red and yellow: 'Be not faithless but believing.'

Michael is suddenly aware of the office in darkness and the room stuffy. He forgets the smell from Don's notes on the desk and floor, shuffles in his seat, and stares out the window at the University lights. A turning tram clangs its bell, a welcome dose of reality. He remembers all this so clearly, thanks to Don's boxes. But the boxes are a can of worms, and Michael recalls his own father's funeral: his mother looking older than her years, in a dark dress with a high collar, a handkerchief held up to her nose, sad eyes that followed the hearse and everything in slow motion, Uncle Kev's meerschaum pipe, the tobacco rich and sweet, the clouds of smoke as he huffed and puffed, piles of pink carnations, the clumps of lilies, pungent and white. Michael rubs his eyes, and imagines himself becoming his builder father, always with his head in a book, always tired, a twinge in his knee, and Jennifer reminding him he never talks.

He takes a deep breath, now thinking of Jennifer in Queensland, doing battle with her father again, only now the twins are all grown. Michael squints, and remembers the twins after their grandad's funeral with wide eyes warning of a bombshell to come: "So Daddie, where's Grandad? What happens when people die?" Always tricky, with Jennifer no help, her pretty nose screwed up: "Ask your father, Melissa." Michael would take the easy way out, his Greeks to the rescue, telling the kids it was like a big sleep, Death being the twin of Sleep of course. But one hurdle would lead to another, like the whys and wherefores of cremation and burying people.

Michael pokes at Don's notes on his desk and pushes the greying curls off his forehead. His thoughts are back at the funeral, gazing around the walls of the Fremantle church. Did Don ever set foot in a church other than the Cathedral at their very last Melbourne meeting? He squinted and waited for the clergyman to finish, his head full of his favourites and Charon the Ferryman - Michael imagining Don standing among a crowd of lost souls on the shore of the river Styx, all waiting to be ferried across this river of forgetfulness. That trip would cleanse them of all earthly troubles, wrongs, and regrets.

Now over twenty years since Don's funeral, Michael flicks on the office lamp and takes in the quiet, the late-night trams and traffic rare. He mulls over Don's notes on his desk, his life and sudden death, the number of times Don had crossed his mind since Peru almost thirty years ago. He wonders what Don would have thought of his PhD. Michael shakes his head. There was never time to raise the subject, not with Don fascinated by the old Aboriginal Missions after Michael's childhood reminiscing that night above Machu Picchu.

Then there is Don's mother, what Michael had been told and what he has now read. He sees her in Don's notes, a powerful influence in his early years. And it dawns on him now, her dread of cremation an odd connection, Michael's

Ferryman insistent on a 'proper' burial; without it, the inno-cent waylaid by evil spirits. "I need a proper night's sleep."

With the church formalities finished, Michael was acutely aware of the open coffin up the front. Robbo was the first to approach the dark rosewood box, Michael feeling even more like an outsider. Don was dead, and Michael did not need to see his body. He had worried about the state of that boyish face, preferring to remember the Don he knew.

It was an odd feeling, Michael suddenly down the front with the others, right there by the coffin. He stood there fidgeting with Don's cards in his vest pocket, his fingers cold on the pressed metal case, staring down at that sleeping face all puffed up and pasty. The familiar tan was gone, the body tucked in a cloistered coffin with walls of red velvet, the white shirt and narrow tie odd and out of kilter. Michael found himself squinting, uneasy at the thought of Don with-out his gold chain.

At the cemetery, Michael pondered the connection with his own life journey so far, the hours of research and those spent browsing through rows of graves, memorials, and monuments, running errands for Clive and chasing family records in Melbourne; the Fremantle Cemetery smaller but just as old, again swallowed by suburbs that grew around the old port. From the car park, he parted with the others. The older section spanned from the 19th Century through to the industrialised era of the 20th. Michael moved through the sea of graves, the headstones a barometer of changing times and the transitions like an open book for him. Things moved away from the individual, the ornate imagery or epitaph less common. He knew without looking at the carved text that it was less likely to be verse, the inscriptions more religious. Yes, there would be expressions of grief, but the notion of death was now largely side-stepped.

Re-joining the group at the gravesite, Michael noted no memorials or monuments, nothing elaborate or special. Instead, he stared along low, neatly clipped rows, the beginning of the garden cemetery set in a simple lawn, the plaques and inscriptions: 'in loving memory' or 'beloved' seeming somehow inadequate and the raised rectangular plinths small and insignificant. Michael remembers the distant traffic, just a hum, a soft shroud of drizzle, the pitter patter on umbrellas, the damp dankness of the newly dug grave, and the surrounding mounds of wet clay and sand. He remembers the lowering of the coffin, not quite taking the words in, his head awash with thoughts of Peru, that first cliff face meeting and the accident.

He stares at the pressed metal case now on his desk. He rubs his eyes, Jennifer having made her view clear more than once: "The boxes of notes? Think of it as a manuscript Michael. Interesting, yes, but nothing to lose sleep over." But then there was The Frenchman, sensing something more, always sceptical of our misplaced sense of entitlement where we must have all the answers and everything under control. "Look, my friend, at what bothers you. *Oui*, it is about not knowing all the answers; something suddenly gone and yet not gone."

And Michael hears Clive's voice too, as plain as day but a tad raspy these days; the frown on his ruddy red face when he signs the receipt for the backroom boxes, the ashtray piled high on his mess of a desk, the stink of his trademark Gauloises cigarettes. "So, Kiddo, you seriously thought that funeral was the end of all this?"

| 39 |

The morning after the funeral, Michael stood with Robbo at the end of Maricielo's street. "Good to get out Mike. Up for a walk?" Michael nodded. They crossed the Fremantle esplanade and strolled in the shade of the Norfolk Pines. "Well... I've been thinking... if you'd like to meet D's father, I mean." Michael stopped mid-stride, Robbo too. "Oh... didn't mean to spring it on you so sudden." He looked back towards the warehouse. "It's just that I couldn't raise it back in front of Angie, and I'm heading off at midday." Michael understood, Angela's thoughts on her father loud and clear. Don had mentioned him briefly, and there was that note on the tree. But even there in Fremantle, he seemed more of a phantom. Robbo motioned to sit on a playground bench. "Look... he's a bloody mess, to be honest."

There was a grimace from Robbo like he was in pain. Michael waited, but Robbo stood without another word. It was clear that Michael was to follow across the Esplanade lawn and railway crossing, then to the deserted waterside restaurants and timber boardwalks. "So sorry, Mike... but look, bear with me, and I'll explain." Robbo scratched the stubble on the side of his face. "It's like this, I guess: you see, he was always on the scene... pretty much right through." Michael frowned. "Yep, I know Mike... D put me in the picture years back. He looked his dad up early on... not long out of school... curious about who he was and why... those family roots again. Visited his dad whenever he could... didn't tell his mum. Too much poison there. Oh, and Angie? How he managed to keep her out of the picture, that's anyone's guess." Robbo stopped in his tracks and grabbed Michael's arm. "Angie can be hard work when she wants to be, and she would be sooo pissed off. Bloody weird though... you saw her Mike... D and her pretty close." Michael did not understand that closeness back then; now, he does. He sees it in Don's notes, Angela a constant presence like an absent twin.

Robbo continues. "Yep... that's it Mike, his dad sorted the funeral himself, but to be honest, I never did expect him to be there. Angie would've crucified him... an ugly, bloody scene for sure. Don's mum never forgave the poor old bugger for leaving... but from where I'm sitting, it was her that kicked him out on his arse."

They paused outside Maricielo's, and Robbo grabbed Michael's elbow. "Angie? She just picked up from where her mum left off, every bit of the vitriol and spite. Never knew why he didn't leave earlier, to be honest... all about the kids, I s'pose."

Robbo had left for the airport when Maricielo glanced

around the living room and dragged Michael out to the courtyard. "*Si*, of course, you must go, Michael; such a nice man. You will see something of Don in him, I think, maybe the eyes." Angela was packing, Michael with the address in his pocket and a quick goodbye, worried at the thought of imposing on Don's father unannounced.

The taxi trip to the outer suburbs reminded Michael of home; the blocks were large, brick houses, some triple-fronted, immaculate lawns, and tidy gardens. He checked the address, paid the driver, and drifted up the driveway, turning at the steps to take in the neighbourhood, the familiar speed humps, no footpaths, no fences, and lawns down to the kerb. Michael had thought of Jennifer and the twins. But there were no signs of kids that he remembers, no scooters lying about, no bikes or bits and pieces. Michael does recall the smell of cut grass and waiting on the porch, again feeling exposed and out of place. The shiny square tiles were spotless, and the timber door of two-tone panels. He rang the doorbell, the chimes seeming drawn out and far too loud.

An older man answered, his back bent and a hobbling gait. His hands trembled. He paused, Michael sure he was being assessed. The greeting was short; Michael directed with one hand to a large open kitchen. He stared across the table as Don's father lowered himself onto a chair; at the far end, a bunch of long-stemmed flowers laid flat, the pink wrapping all wet. Michael wondered at his age, probably taller when younger but no more than sixty years old, with weary eyes the same brown as Don's.

| **40** |

Michael again surprises himself, recalling that empty stare from over twenty years ago: meeting Don's father only that once, his life broken by the death of his son and both fists clenched on the table. The older man finally nodded and raised his hands. "Don't worry Michael, I know about you and your meetings. He told me. And I know about you being a historian, helping him find his way to wherever he was heading. It means a lot to me."

Don's father continued and the best Michael could manage was a weak smile. "Yes, I bet this must seem complicated. You see, I thought I'd lost everything when I finally left, but Don found me, not the other way around. Still a teen when he sought me out. He'd asked about me in Freo." The older man shook his head. "Not his mother, of course, never his mother. She would've been furious. And Angela? Just a girl back then, but I'm sure you know the story there."

Don's father looked up. Michael was startled by a younger woman in the kitchen doorway. She asked if Michael wanted a drink and handed him a beer, a glass and a bottle of rum for Don's father. She left as quietly as she arrived, Don's father more open by his third rum, "Don had finished with school when he first dropped by. A shock, really, but wonderful to see him growing up. But then the wandering started of course, his grandad's genes, him from over your way, eventually turning up here, just outside Kalgoorlie. That's what I told Don. But I could tell he was disappointed, me not knowing much at all. I never guessed that would be the order of things in the end. I guess he just filled in the gaps himself until you came along, and then went on from there."

"Anyway, there was work up north at the mine; Robbo's idea. Unlike Angela, Don would never be an academic or anything like that. More like me I suppose." Michael gets it now, from Don's notes, escaping his mother's orbit and the beginnings of another life, real or imagined. Don's father had shrugged, composing his thoughts. "Something got to Don around about that time. He talked about this bloke at the mine, the land, and the way he just knew things. Obviously, a big thing."

Michael shuffles the notes on his office desk, younger back then and always surprised when strangers confided in him. He knew Don's father was nervous and yet comfortable enough to talk and confirm his son's fascination with Michael's childhood country upbringing.

"But Michael, I reckon the mine had something to do with that change, even before you came along. I saw it. But first, there were his mother's demons to deal with, enough of them to sink a ship. And that took him to France for sure. Then there was Maricielo, a real chance there, or so I hoped. Only let his guard down once. Said he could never get close to anyone."

Don's father had demolished rum number four. "This

accident Michael. I must identify my son. So I go to Melbourne, 'traumatic asphyxia' they say." Michael had shuffled in his seat and fiddled with Don's cards in his vest pocket. "Just horrific, me in the morgue, I mean, the white sheet pulled away. I hardly know my own son."

Michael sensed the older man drifting through what had happened in his head, sorting things as he went, filing each piece away and trying to push forward. He wonders if that was the first time Don's father had spoken about the accident. "It's a young woman who finds him first, Michael. I feel so sorry for her. She's walking her dog in the dark. It is she who rings the ambulance. The police take photographs, search the site and find nothing untoward. But the Melbourne coroner holds up the funeral, so I wait. These things take days."

Don's father stared into his empty glass. "It's the ambulance driver who declares he's dead. My son. Still can't get my head around it." His eyes met Michael's. "You saw it Michael? The tree that did this?" Yes, Michael saw it, and it still bothers him after twenty-two years; the bleeding sap stuck to his fingertips and the cuff of his Paisley shirt, the smell of damp grass and sawdust, the wet note at the base, and the flowers. He imagines Don's father repeating that same story over and over, just as Michael had and still does.

Michael sat in silence, Don's father with both hands on the table, fingers and words trembling. "The tree is old Michael, the branch hitting him across the back of his shoulders, his legs buckling under the impact." He stops, with eyes like glass fixed on the centre of the table. "I tried to contact her, the woman who found him. But I know it's tough, her not wanting to talk to an old man like me."

He fell silent; Michael was surprised by the woman re-appearing to sit next to him. She spoke with eyes averted to the flowers at the far end of the table. He remembers the wilting hand on his shoulder, the rings on one finger, the loud sigh, and the International accent. "My name is Isabelle, and it is you only and Mr Robbo who are visitors." She extends one hand across the table to Don's father, his eyes down. "There are no friends since we marry. And now Mr Michael, it is difficult for me to get him from bed. He does not eat, little sleep." She sighed again, tears down her chin and chest. "I have bought him these." She nodded to the bunch of lilies, the pink paper sopping wet.

All three sat through a pregnant pause until Don's father picked up the story again. "I know from the start Don is too close to his mother. And she really was something else: those mood swings, odd ways, the cards and stories to fill his head with God knows what. But I feel it, especially now, the lost chance at a real family connection; Don and Angela, my kids, after all." Michael remembers staring again, the flowers spicy and sweet, Isabelle pushing her chair closer and taking the left hand of Don's father, rubbing his fingers gently between her palms, seeming to give him the strength to go on.

"Well Michael, after Freo I wasn't sure what to do; one or two church friends were still there back then. And the kids, of course, but me not welcome. The suburbs here didn't seem that far away. Don was five years old, and Angela was just four. A different place back then, those narrow Freo roads and dead ends, everything pokey and run down." His eyes wandered. "I bought this place new and met Isabelle later."

He smiled for the first time. "A life less complicated. But now I'm stuck in the past."

"So, I'm back in Freo Michael, that woman soon to be the mother of my kids. She's an open book at first, or so I thought." Michael detected a half smile. "Even with the black lipstick. She's an only child, vivacious but paranoid that her family name would disappear." He had tapped his fingers on the table. "Crazy. Still don't get it to this day." He raised his hand to make a point. "So, about the family name: she wants the kids to keep it." He peered into the bottom of his glass of rum. "The only argument I ever won." He dropped his chin and stared down at his and Isabelle's hand on the table. Michael asked about Don's Christian name; the immediate answer was a deep breath. "Ah, that. Yes, Michael, her idea." Michael had stared at the bunch of lilies limp on the table, then back at Don's father.

"French? Yes. You bet; me just a simple man from the wrong side of the track and suddenly out of my depth with an exotic creature I hardly know. But I'm the first to admit she had a tough time. I put it down to jealousy, her so beautiful, too different for the good folk of Freo in those days."

"I suppose it started badly with my church friends deciding she was Catholic." He shook his head. "She never said. Anyway, it didn't matter one iota in the end."

"I was infatuated in those days; as simple as that. I lived and breathed for that lavender scent, needing to know everything about her. At first, she talked. Said her grandfather took her aside when she was little, skeletons in the closet from way back, the family escaping the south of France to a poorer but safer life up north. Some to the north of Italy. Her parents drowned in a lake somewhere. No living relatives left that she knew of, something she went on and on about."

"Anyway, that's it, in a nutshell, Michael, her jumping on a boat the first chance she gets and landing here." Michael raised his eyebrows, "Yes, an unusual choice, maybe. Who knows? I remember her teeth like pearls. She laughed in those days, pulled out a small camphorwood box lined with royal blue velvet, her mum's tortoiseshell hair combes, and that little tin case of cards she dumped on Don for his sixteenth birthday. Oh yes, and some photos of The Blue Mountains, courtesy of some shifty French travel agent selling Australia as the ideal holiday destination; the other side of the country, of course."

"Later, she just clams up, and things get nasty." He shook his head. "Told me to get lost. Look, I've no idea what happened, but it wasn't exactly sudden."

"So Michael, I'm gone for less than a year, and she changes the kids' surnames to her family name, me well and truly out of it by then. So there, the argument I first won, but lost the war in the end."

"From then on, it was all about Don for me." The older man's eyes narrowed at each mention of his son. "The writing? Important to him from the early days. The suggestion of a teacher who thought he was struggling. It may have gotten a bit out of hand, I suppose. But he said he just had to, and that was the end of it. Not many friends that I could see, but then I wasn't around for long. There was a young kid called Gracie way back in primary school. There is Robbo, of course, and for a while, Maricielo." He stares down at the tabletop. "Don.

Always a dreamer, all-night reading marathons and later, those cards. He showed me once."

Michael was suddenly aware of the cards heavy in his pocket. He gently dropped the metal card case on the table and explained where he had found the chain. Don's father sighed, surprised, but seemed relieved. "I did wonder about the cards and chain, the cards from his mother of course. And I'm so very glad that Maricielo has the chain. I did try to change his mind about that wonderful girl, talk some sense into him, Robbo too from memory. But no hope there. I just didn't get it after all the work on that warehouse. He always was a bit distant, but I hoped he might at least feel something. But no, there was always another quest, this time all about my father."

"After his stint at the mine, I thought there might be light at the end of the tunnel, finally breaking away from that woman's spell. He'd started asking me questions about my side of things, family stuff, and the like. There's not a lot to it though Michael: bits about my father and Goldfields map from over your way." He took another gulp of rum. "Well, not much more I could tell him, me dumped in a foster family as a kid over Kalgoorlie way."

"To be honest, I was always petrified Angela would find out about his visits, I mean. She did eventually, of course, and Maricielo copped a blast, all hell breaking loose when I flew to Melbourne to identify Don's body. Then there was the funeral." Isabelle refilled his glass. "One of his last visits was when he'd left Maricielo."

"He was good with his hands, do-it-yourself stuff. So that was an in for me, I guess. I helped him with whatever he needed, loads of my tools in the back of that wagon. I knew it was tricky for him, us a big secret, him dropping by after work, and then, later on, whenever in town."

"You know Michael, I passed the old Freo place from time to time, falling down around their ears." Isabelle pressed his hand, and Michael was surprised at his skinny fingers, his skin grey and translucent, the face frail and already worn out. Don's father had coughed as if clearing his throat. "The woman I married was a strange one, and I didn't see any of it coming." His eyes dropped to his hands on the table. "And I still miss the lavender."

| 41 |

Michael stares down at his desk and the handful of Don's earliest notes given to him by Maricielo before the funeral. His eyes fix on the top page with the `DDA' included in the header; Don's writing is so much like his father's. But these first stories are his mother's: of her early classes at the Fremantle Art Centre, the upright easels, stools and benches, a fireplace that crackled and spat but the room was still so cold. And to Michael, these stories seem more relevant now, Don's take on Fremantle when just a kid, and Maricielo insisting that Michael visit the Arts Centre after the funeral and before heading home.

After meeting Don's father, Michael had wandered the streets for a while, pondering all the older man had said: ambling along The Cappuccino strip to Don's Roundhouse and Bathers' Beach, then the historic Prison, Town Hall, and lastly, the Arts Centre itself. He remembers his guide 'William,' a balding retiree in a safari jacket and a big badge saying 'ask me'; the two of them standing on a Fremantle street. Michael had gazed up at the gables and arched entrances, glancing across at his guide; the traffic was far too close, and a bus belching black smoke stank to high heaven.

William cleared his throat. "Now, you are a historian. So, let me tell you something about this place, young man, our Museum and Arts Centre, our pride and joy. Firstly, we will need to go back a piece – to 1864 – this same building, the colony's first lunatic asylum, was built of limestone and left-overs from wrecked convict ships. Prison labour, of course." Michael had nodded his head. Yes, the building was interesting, the entire length of limestone, the colonnades stylish, the proportions clever, and the emphasis on height, all over-looking Fremantle proper.

William had leaned to one side and pointed to the wall. "There were additions over the years, some ramshackle mods to accommodate deranged male and female convicts, the colony's growing numbers of mentally ill."

"That all ended with overcrowding and complaints, poor treatment and deaths, then an inquiry. The place was condemned as unhealthy and unsafe." His voice dropped to a whisper. "Nasty stuff, with another ten years before they shut it down and rescued any poor sods left. And I'll tell you something. It can get weird here, the cleaners with their own stories. And sometimes I think, why the heck not, with a history like this? If there are ghosts in Freo, I reckon they'd be here for sure."

Michael ran one hand along the sandstone wall, stood back, and blew the dust off his fingers, imagining Don's mother whispering stories in an impressionable young son's ear, William watching him like a hawk. "Now, where were we young man? Ah yes; next, there was the Women's home from 1909 to 1941, impossibly overcrowded again, shocking conditions, cruel, and you guessed it, more unexplained deaths.

But for me, it's the next stage I find the most interesting, you too, by the sound of it. But I have a personal connection, my uncle, at school here back in the day." Michael squinted. "Yeah, absolutely true, right here, a Technical School of all things. Crazy, yes? Just after the war from 1946 through to '55, my Uncle Jack on about it after too many ports. He'd talk about how freezing it was all year round, blazing fires the only heating, but still abysmally cold. Saw him a couple of times a year. He'd roll up his sleeve like a party trick, a white weal of a scar from elbow to wrist. Said it happened right here in class, one night while studying; an invisible knife cut him with no one near, and the school condemned shortly after. Yes, I bet there's been some crazy stuff happen here."

"So, that gets us to the here and now. There's a transformation; to this magnificent Museum and Arts Centre from 1973 on." Michael remembers feeling odd, with a tingle at the back of his neck. He was standing in the middle of that big room, Don's mother finally real, a slight woman over by the wall. She was a worrier from what he now knows from these boxes; her hair was long and straight, pitch black, that family tortoiseshell combe at the back of her head, and black lips. The hand-knitted shawl would have been black, draped over rakish shoulders and held to her chest with a small pale hand, a waft of lavender, and a wooden potters' wheel, the cold mound of clay rock hard and impossible to mould. The long skirt would have been black and down to the floor.

Don's first notes are still here on the desk, the young writer's 1980 mentions of his mother: the mystery footsteps, unseen hands scaring frightened students, and William on about the cruelty, the reoccurring mistreatment, so many murders and suicides.

Michael leans back in his office chair and stares across at Clive's empty desk. He squints, the notes leading him once more: Don's sister and enigmatic mother, Don the wanderer with a head full of stories, Angela's bravado that had quickly peeled away, the bleach blonde hair and dark roots, the clunky bangle that rattled when she raised her glass or cigarette. He hopes she has finally forgiven her father but somehow doubts it.

| **42** |

Michael's thoughts have finally moved on from Fremantle, the funeral and Don's father, but he has several stacks of Don's notes still to process. The notes on his desk are shuffled in line with the dates at the top of the page. He leans to the side and inspects the carpet, covered in sheets he has discarded over the last week, the blank and impossibly damaged. He cannot believe this thing may be coming to an end.

• January 1994/The Albert, Melbourne Bayside

I'm on the first floor of the pub, the south side, a long passage to the end, the door a fire escape, the carpet black & burgundy. The room's big enough, the small corner table my desk, does the job, a home for my scribbles, a kettle & cup. The single bed is waste high, the cast ends tall, a skinny wardrobe with two doors. There's a bedspread like Mama's, crocheted red, blue & white. The table lamp is brass, a girl in a long clinging dress.

I'm here for a while longer, a bit like Freo, a sign that flickers by the corner door, neon red, rooms for rent, the outside whitish, flakes of paint faded & falling, raised letters up high, the pub name unreadable, the front wall facing a sunset bay. Down the side is the red brick wing, the German's room & mine.

I drag myself down to the empty bar, listen to the German & smoke some spliffs. I'm working long hours & half listening till I move to the window, poke my head out the door and stare past palm fronds that wave in salty sea air. Across the water wharf lights flicker.

Later I sit in my room, one card with a desert backdrop. I think of Kelvin, but the whisper is Mama's – *Oui*, here is a woman with a great lion. She wears a crown of flowers, a matching belt, plain pale dress & bare feet. She leans forward, gently holds the lion's head, tilts it back until the beast's mouth is wide open.

& I do feel I'm in control, or getting there, ready for another move & getting some cash together, heading off on my 60 minute route march to work each day, through back-streets & parks, a stranded strip of shops from gold rush days. Shopfronts are dark, verandahs wide, street lamps aglow, the shadows of iron trim & ornate cast posts.

• **February 1994/The Albert, Melbourne Bayside**

The cloisters are dusty from an always quarter open window, the warm air balmy. Mostly I scribble, or lay awake listening, the traffic lights, the click when they change. The curtains barely move in the briskest breeze. There's a fire escape outside, covered in cobwebs, rusted steel down to a cracked concrete carpark, Gracie sad & sorry, fading bonnet beneath the landing, out of sight, out of mind, an embarrassment like me Siss. I'm stuffed after working all night, but still scribbling, with another box for Robbo's garage.

• March 1994/The Albert, Melbourne Bayside

The table's crowded, the busted satchel a paperweight, my emptied pockets' keys & coins, a pile of scribbles, some on the floor. The stories still come in fits & starts, the changing tide, more missing pieces. No luck with Mama's family, no answers, why I'm half here & half there. I've Michael's books I should return.

Cards are spread on the bed & I pick one, a hint of lavender from the crocheted bedspread – You see this man? *Oui*, tall, in robes, a crown of gold. See him addressing the crowd? A carved column on either side, a set of keys at his feet, a staff in his left hand. You must know the truth is based on reason Donatien, collecting the facts, what you know & do not.

Well Siss, she would never approve of where I'm at right now. But I open the map, about 100 or so kilometres Dad said, within sight of some old volcano, but never been anywhere himself. I lean close, this inkblot on the map, right on the highway, an intersection of lines, somewhere to start, loading up Gracie for a trip that may come to nothing. It's time & we'll be back here for work on Monday.

| **43** |

Maria is not often at the café these days, but today holds forth from behind the coffee machine, joking with regulars but with one eye on Michael. Her head bobs when she laughs or flicks the lever. Michael sits tucked in a corner, the same blue jeans as always, the same Paisley shirt and corduroy vest. He scratches the side of his head, the mess of curls greyer these days. Next to his folded newspaper is a squarish plate with a single *pignoli* cookie.

He has known Maria since before Don's death and feels she is always ready to pounce. Now she is by his table, hands on hips, demanding to know how far he has gotten with Don's boxes. "Well, Lover, we see so little of you these days. You have some news? No secrets please." Michael shrugs, and she follows him to the door. "I see now. This thing, it is more than the cards. But Lover, you must let your Maria help and must not worry all of the time." Michael promises he will, and she squeezes his arm before he breaks away and heads for the office.

Today he knows Clive will be waiting, supposedly retired, and the backroom boxes like a magnet. Michael squints. Clive always said the funeral would not be the end of this, clearly disappointed at Michael packing the whole thing away after the funeral. And Michael is apprehensive, Clive still larger than life, the Gauloises and overflowing ashtray left behind on his rare visits these days. Michael can hear his old boss's baiting already: "So Kiddo, what's with the boxes?" He can already see the raised eyebrows, the Andy Warhol mop of hair.

Closer to the office, he stops at one street-side elm, his hand on the bark, the vertical furrows grey, cold and rough. Finally, at the gate, he stands and turns, gazes across the road at the University, the clang of changing trams killing the hum of morning traffic. As expected, Clive is waiting inside and obviously excited that Don is finally back on the agenda after all these years. Michael smiles to himself, rarely crosses paths with his old boss these days, after working in each other's pockets for so long. Michael squints. It takes some adjustment; Clive's beat-up tweed jacket is finally consigned to the charity clothes bin. His face is craggier these days, with a powder pink cardigan the order of the day, although paired with the ubiquitous moleskins.

It is all about the boxes now. "That stink does take the cake, Kiddo." But then Clive goes quiet, lambchop sideburns lifting with a wan smile. Michael pulls at his chair, sits back to his desk, and faces Clive. But there is no taunting today, no wind-ups, Clive simply asking to be bought up to speed on the latest notes. He listens in silence right to the end, one Gauloises after another stubbed in the piled-up ashtray. He stares past Michael and out the window, the smoke making Michael cough. For him, this is a different Clive, not the same boss that prodded him to go to the funeral twenty-two years ago, to meet family and friends for some sort of closure, a closure that never really happened.

And now, Michael was back at the same point, the cards again in his pocket thanks to these newly inherited boxes, and at least some of the questions answered. Don had left Maricielo for Melbourne, sharing a house, Robbo married, and Don moved to The Albert Hotel at Robbo's suggestion. Michael waits as Clive stubs another butt in the ashtray. "So, Kiddo, you know more than you did back then, and that's a fact."

"Look, I know you wanted to leave it behind. I get that. But now you have the tools, these boxes are the key. So, what about Don's last digs? Do we have anything on his time at The Albert?" Michael frowns, and Clive takes a deep breath. "Well? I'd be looking at that, the known unknowns. I'd be wondering what he was up to, why he was there, why the back and forth. Come on Kiddo, don't you feel just a twinge of curiosity? I mean, is there no room for just a little mystery in that straight-laced life of yours?" He scratches his sideburns, and Michael shrugs. He recalls Don's dream, a distressed young girl in that bleak-sounding hotel room the night before the accident. Clive is the same old boss, but looking invigorated, excited almost, that still like straw but now peppered with grey.

"And we've been here before Kiddo, have we not? The secret is to have a serious go at finding answers this time, or just forget it and move on. I'm just saying. There's no way I could leave something like this and just slip back to normal. You've got the chance of a lifetime with these boxes, and I know you, Kiddo, you and your loose ends."

"So, how to proceed? Look, I suggest you consider it a job, the stuff you've been doing for thirty years. Can you believe that?" He stops and again stares past Michael and out the office window. "Have to agree with The Frenchman on that one. There are answers here for those that look."

Michael drives across town to the bay, stands by his parked car on the footpath across from The Albert, stares out across the bluestone seawall, then up and down a promenade of palms, the fronds brown and burned. Most of the tree guards are crooked or broken. He turns with the beach and bay breeze at his back. He gazes across the traffic and up at the ornate corner tower. He wonders how much the place has changed; already old when Don lived here but still quite something, and seen from up and down the entire beach-front. He inspects the detail, 19th Century but rundown, the tower an octagonal-crowned rarity with a pointed roof. He jogs across the road between traffic, the tower looming high above the corner bar, the triple-storey facade imposing.

Greek-style colonnades are directly in front, Michael standing still and staring up. He squints, the frontage elaborate but tired. He turns away and walks around the corner; a plain wing of red brick extends to a driveway. A rusted fire escape rises from the empty courtyard with clumps of weeds between cobbles and concrete. He turns again, and then it's back to the corner, stepping up between the entrance colonnades and finally inside the foyer. His eyes wander, the original elegance still there, the entry spacious, the traffic noise drowned out, the timber tarnished and dark, the red-carpet steps threadbare. He now doubts there has been much change since Don came and went. He sniffs the air, the same musty smell as Clive's office.

The barman is Andreas, a talker who nods when he speaks. Michael stares at a face too pale and a stringy mane of greasy grey hair. "Mmmm, *Ja*; it brings back the memories. A long time gone, and me just finished with backpacking and the Hare Krishnas. I'm still here, of course, but can't forget this strange man that always wants the same room." The barman looks up to the ceiling. "It needs repairs back then, still does. But it never bothers him. There were plans for the building, but never any money. Maybe it is difficult to know where to begin." Andreas leans on the bar and shakes his head, his face closer to Michael. "Look, I never judge, but I remember."

Michael watches the barman twirl a lock of his hair

between finger and thumb, then peer around the bar. "So, there is history here, and I know a part. And I still think about this after all these years. I mean, this man is new back then, but how much does he actually know?" Michael squints at the question and fumbles with the cards in his pocket. The German pours two beers. "First, I must tell you something of this place. Once, there were nuns who lived here, *ja*, a safe house for young women, some just kids of fifteen years old. So, that is the story I know."

"He mostly comes and goes in the dark, the bakery I think, his *auto* parked out back. But I don't see him every day." Andreas shakes his head, eyes on the beers. "*Ja*, he is in the bar sometime; no beer for him though. We smoke some grass, and he talks a little. Me, my room is close, the same wing." Andreas waves an arm towards the side street. "The red brick, we call it the 'new' wing, haha. I am living at this end, close to the stairs and the bar. His room is there too, but the other end from mine and close to the fire escape outside, his *auto* under the landing." He pulls a set of keys off the wall and hands them over. "You will see his room."

Michael leaves his half-finished beer and pockets the keys with a pink plastic tag. He wanders back to the foyer and up the stairs. The floorboards creak under his desert boots, the stair risers unequal and awkward, steep and winding. The wooden balustrades are smooth, black, and bulky. He stops at the level one landing, gazes around, squints, and steps down.

The levels don't match, the narrow-panelled door half hidden behind an alcove wall, the 'new wing' entry easily missed. He wonders how many lost themselves in this quaint old place over the years, missing this level and drifting up the tower to the next, then left meandering about until returning to Andreas for directions. Michael pushes at the door. But then, how many visitors would a neglected place like this have?

He finally stands in the new wing gazing down the length of the central hallway. He sniffs the dust, more panelled doors equally spaced on both sides, the single light globe dull, the walls blotchy, the carpet and painted timber dark. His eyes are drawn to the door at the far end, a faint green light above that marks the fire escape. The floor squeaks as he passes Andreas' room first, the shared bathroom and toilets, and further along, the last room with a hole in the door the size of a twenty-cent piece; the old lock removed, the new knob and keyhole higher.

Michael turns the key, pushes, and flicks the porcelain light switch with a loud click. Don's room is on the south side, square and dark, the ceiling high. Cloistered curtains are a dusty shade of claret, the heavy folds hanging from top to floor. He looks up; the ceiling rose a wreath of leaves and blossoms, a long cord down to a woven red light shade, the fringe frayed. And the old feeling is back, the tingle on the back of his neck, Michael not comfortable at being here. He stares at the high single bed, the heavy iron frame at both ends, the crocheted bedspread smelling like old socks. His nose twitches. "Yes, and just a dash of lavender." The single pillow is plain and flat. He scratches his head. Has the room been empty since the accident over twenty years ago?

The curtains crowd a plastic kettle and cup on a squarish desk of a table. On the floor is a singular lamp, the brass figure of a slim woman in a long dress that clings to her hips and legs, the hem spread to make a stable base. Michael pushes aside a low three-legged stool with one hand. He leans down and picks up the lamp. His fingers wrap around the statue's legs, the brass rippled, smooth, and cold: Art Nouveau and possibly French. He wishes Clive was here to see this and holds it up in the feeble light. She is tall, arms bare and stretched above her head. She leans slightly back, both hands clasping a flower held high and pointed forward and down like a torch, the small pointed globe a stamen. Michael peers closer, one petal cracked.

He cocks his head to one side and thinks of Don alone and writing, the peak hour traffic a dull hum. He steps past the bed and towards the window, pushes aside the curtains, and coughs; the clack of curtain rings from a wooden rod high on the wall. Michael tugs at the window latch and pulls harder, the wooden frame double-hung and heavy. He pushes up, the frame groans, and the window is open. There is a blast of air and the rush of traffic, a whiff of sea salt, and the cry of gulls. He turns to the bay and imagines living here, in this backwater of a place, Don keeping his odd hours, propped on this stool, the table tiny, writing in the light of this lamp. There would always be traffic at peak hour and beachgoers in summer, the side street island with a rundown red brick restaurant that looks more like a Victorian toilet block. He squints and imagines the click of pedestrian traffic lights in the middle of the night.

He returns the keys to the barman, guzzles the last of his beer, and waits. "So, you see the place. *Ja*, it is mostly just him and me, and I don't think he ever sleeps. I look down the passage and see the light under the door in the daytime when I go to the bathroom. I hear the rustle of paper, the floor that squeaks. In the bar, it is mostly me that is talking. We smoke a load of grass in those days." Andreas smiles. "Once, I ask him about his papers, what he writes. I think it is a diary." Michael lifts himself off his bar stool and leans closer.

"Well, I am the cleaner also, once every week. I find his papers on the floor and the bed, putting them back on his table to make things tidy." Andreas tops up both beers. "But no, as I say, I never read anything. This is private, he is private, but sometimes I see the dates, sometimes the place names at the top of the page." Andreas drains his beer and runs one hand through his hair. "So, I ask him, just once. He is embarrassed and calls them scribbles. No more asking."

| 44 |

Jennifer is finally back from Queensland. Michael slumps in his favourite chair after dinner, Jennifer on the couch and her book closed. "Well darling, that's the family sorted." Michael detects a smirk, and she tosses her head to the side, that torrent of grey hair with just a hint of red these days. "Now, I understand, Michael darling, I do; why this thing is so personal, these boxes the bitter end. And I know you; needing to have all the answers all the time. The way I see it, that's the crux of the whole thing. And about this dream, that skinny ghost of a girl in blue; well, sorry, it makes my skin crawl."

He squints and agrees it is odd, but Don's notes are loaded with stories. Michael knows all too well that Jennifer has had enough and desperately wants him to move on.

Michael arrives at the office early. Clive is there again, and Michael suspects he is keen for an update on Don's time at The Albert. But Clive has other things on his mind, his desk more of a mess than the old days, loaded with books, pamphlets, and papers dug up from the University library.

Michael takes a deep breath, runs through the latest for Clive, and waits for the interruption that never comes. Clive just sits there blowing smoke rings and picks at his cardigan sleeve. "Well, Kiddo, where to start? Let's forget about your known knowns for just one minute. With your friend's notes, you've got plenty to work with, plenty of what makes this guy tick. We could start with his later notes, something you have a handle on, something from when you yourself were a kid: our Indigenous folk and their relationship with the land. You say his notes are more and more into that stuff. And we could talk about your friend's sense of place and this vibration thing."

Michael is concerned about superstition hijacking everything and is apprehensive; Clive and The Frenchman are a formidable tag team. "Look Kiddo..." Clive abruptly stops, one hand settling on Michael's shoulder. He seems to be reassessing something and Michael wonders what is up. "Look, Michael, we are just trying to help, with more to life than your 'bricks and mortar.' You didn't see it back then, but we've got his notes now, boxes of them, and maybe there's something you're missing. Now, let's just say we fast-forward to modern times and more contemporary thinkers like the American William Burroughs: anything can have a spirit of some sort: a valley, a house, or a simple block of stone."

Michael squints and shuffles in his seat, wondering what a drug addict writer has to do with this and where the discussion is going. Clive takes a deep breath. "OK. I know, a modern take on things? Well, maybe not so modern. Burroughs claimed that the nature of these spirits is that they can remain forever. Sound familiar? An idea that's been around since the dawn of time Michael. Drifts in and out of your friend's stories, of course. And yes, I have been yacking to The Frenchman about this. That man is difficult to ignore at the best of times."

Clive falls silent, one puff after another, holding his cigarette at arm's length, his eyes on it as if it might burst into flame at any moment. Michael braces himself, waiting. "OK, if you don't like that one Michael, let's talk about the elephant in the room. It's about that dream." Clive runs a finger through his muttonchop sideburns, the two men facing each other. "I agree with Jennifer on that one: the blue robes, the smoke, and the wet floor. Pretty intense, don't you think? Too colourful a description to just pick from thin air?"

Michael has already dissected the dream more than once, Jennifer making sure of that. But Don was a writer, a prolific reader, and with no monopoly on imagination. And the boxes had a load of stories just as imaginative as that dream. Michael squints and thinks he has heard it all, but his old boss has been busy. "That dream written down in his hotel room, I believe. And hell Michael, this is his final entry if I'm not mistaken, the poor guy dead within twenty-four hours. Well, I've done some homework."

Clive's desk has one book bigger than the others. Michael

squints at the hefty volume of French history, then the pamphlets and papers in piles, all alongside a bottle of brandy, two glasses, and Clive's heaped ashtray perched precariously at the end. Michael is not surprised at Clive's fascination with any perceived French connection and wonders if his old boss has slept in the office. "Now, Michael, hang on, humour me, please. About this dream. It seems to me we're talking known unknowns at worst."

Michael takes a deep breath, and Clive's eyes narrow. "I'll tell you something about dreams. Been reading this paper here after chatting with Jennifer. Yes, she rang me. And yes, she is worried about you." He prods at the chaos on his desk, cigarette ash falling to the ancient Axminster. "And don't tell me you don't care." Clive pours two brandies, and Michael looks at his watch. He ponders how Clive has changed, continually poking Michael and showing no mercy in the old days. But now, seemingly wanting to help.

"About this French thing. Know anything about reincarnation?" Michael rolls his eyes, his old boss not waiting for an answer. "Well, try this on for size, a true story about another dream, well, hypnosis really: An English psychiatrist is impressed with a woman patient's 'uncanny accuracy' when talking of Medieval French times: odd stuff like poems, table utensils, the layout of a Medieval castle where some serious stuff went down. She talks of ceremonies and rituals; being the lover of a priest from a Christian sect, both of them being interrogated and burned at the stake."

Michael notes the wry smile, Clive enjoying himself, thumbing through a pamphlet until stopping at the page he wants, reading directly from the next, another flake of ash floating to the floor. "Now, get this Michael: her detailed description: 'I didn't know that when you burn to death, you'd bleed. I thought the blood would all dry up in the terrible heat. But I was bleeding heavily. The blood was dripping and hissing in the flames. I wished I had enough blood to put the flames out. The worst part was my eyes... I tried to close my eyelids but I couldn't. They must have been burned off...'"

The cards are heavy in Michael's vest pocket, and he wonders if Clive has lost it, maybe the early onset of Alzheimer's or something. But there was no stopping his old boss. "Yes, I know. Damn morbid, but that woman's dream meant something, the stuff about the poems I mean, the utensils, the castle, ceremonies and rituals, all animals endowed with reason and not to be eaten, the patient insisting 'the priest wore dark blue robes'." Clive's eyes leave his desk and stare directly at Michael.

"But here's the thing, something else to take in: it's another twenty years before all that is proved to be true from newly-discovered texts, that same Christian sect found to wear blue." Clive stops, closes the pamphlet, and stares at Michael. "But I know you Michael, not necessarily swayed by that sort of thing. Well, here's something else to go on with: your friend's people from the south of France on his mother's side. Am I right there?" Michael concedes with a nod, pouts, and fumbles with Don's cards.

"So, let me tell you about that part of the world, the beginnings of modern France, the long periods of chaos, nasty stuff, never-ending wars, and bubonic plague." Michael knows this Clive all too well, the old Clive back, peppering his narrative with dates, facts, and figures. And again, he cannot help suspecting the familiar hand of The Frenchman. "Just saying, Michael. Let's assume Don's people did in fact, come from the south; a big move in those days, walking the only option for the greater population. So, we're talking about some massive social or natural upheaval for sure: a tectonic shift of social norms."

Michael is listening and just maybe, after all that has happened, is a little more willing to accept there are things in the world he does not understand. But in the end, he is a realist and sceptical of Clive, his imagination, and those unknown-unknowns. As Michael sees it, science will get there in the end, with religion, superstition, and black magic eventually relegated to the rubbish heap. "OK, Michael. We've known each other for over thirty years. Right?" Michael nods.

"Well, I reckon The Frenchman and I can read you like a book. A historian, first and foremost, your dad a builder. Right? So, let's get into some history; just putting it out there. I'm talking history of the Modern French ilk, the Catholic Church a big part of the whole shebang." He stops, glances at Michael, and takes a slurp of brandy. "Interesting. From what

I recall, your friend Don has no time for the Catholic Church. Anyway, we're talking 10th to 11th Century, for starters."

Michael is bemused at Clive obviously in his element. "Look Michael, stick with me; it's important. We're in Medieval France, towns growing into urban centres, the church's wealth and power increasing, and the break between the Catholic and Orthodox in the 11th Century. To the Orthodox side, the Catholics are barbarous and incapable of serious discussion. But I digress. Let's stick to France: urban centres as Feudal states. Next, we are in the 12th Century, alliances divided, and civil wars commonplace. And this Michael, is where things get really interesting from where I'm sitting, the good people of the south with their own language and, heaven forbid, their own take on religion. They call themselves *Cathari*."

"The year is 1179, and I'm returning to our theory here; things are getting a touch intense. We have a Pope happy to tackle the growing problem of these Christian heretics in the south - the Cathar Heresy - and within 30 years, we have a Holy Crusade; the very first against other Christians." Clive stops and fills Michael's glass with another brandy.

"Well, this Cathar lot are a small minority, not happy with the excesses and power of the Catholic Church. And who could blame them? But their rules for men and women Priests are strict: no sex as it promotes physical existence, a bad thing in their books. For the rest of the population though, it's not so tough, living normal lives pending an absolution from sin before death: a last right of sorts. Oh yes, and remember that stuff about blue robes? They wore blue Michael. They really did." Clive blows another smoke ring.

"The truth is these guys are gentle folk, vegetarian, and highly respected locally. The towns are walled, the Cathar numbers small, the Crusader knights laying siege outside and encouraged by the Papal promise of all the booty and land they want. But there's a problem. Imagine a group of armoured ruffians, camped outside the walls, but the population inside looks all the same. How can the actual Cathar heretics be recognised? Of course, there's an answer, a Papal decree that everyone inside the walls is killed, as 'God will recognise his own.' Absolute political genius!"

"Now, in case we doubt how bad things were, let's go on a trip to 1209, a town called Beziers." Clive taps one of the volumes on his desk. "These Holy Crusaders break through the defences, the men of the town up on the walls, women, children and the elderly inside the churches; seven thousand inside St. Mary Magdalene church with Catholic Priests at the altar." Clive drops a butt on the ashtray and more ash on the carpet. "Every single soul in that church is killed, the floor awash with blood."

"And what does the Papal Emissary say to that? Well, he says the town's capture is 'miraculous', fifteen thousand townsfolk of all religions, all ages, and sex all slaughtered. Surviving prisoners are mutilated and used for target practice. On top of that, all are Catholics except for two hundred."

"So, again, Michael my boy, what I'm pushing here is the intensity of the whole thing, your friend's 'power of place'. I'm talking about this terror, the Darkest Ages in the south of France. And this stuff goes on and on, all here in the history books. After the first town, the Crusaders capture the second. Hundreds of prisoners are bound together and set on the road, all in a line, each one with both eyes gouged out except for the leader. There's wholesale murder, mayham, and gross mutilation from the east across the entire south of France. Our sect of heretics is pretty much broken by the middle of the 13th Century, a civilian exodus big time."

There is the screech of a braking tram outside the office, Michael admitting Clive's musings are gory but fascinating, but then history can be like that. It had been a while, and Michael had forgotten how his old boss could spin a yarn, like all those times he held forth in The Prince Hotel, the long liquid lunches, the late Friday nights, and Michael's lost weekends recovering. That was before the kids.

But Clive is not finished. "Still with me Michael? We're up to 1229, the birth of The Inquisition. travelling far and wide, branching out and harassing anyone thought different."

"The numbers? Well, this is something else we do know about; the Catholics nothing if not good record keepers, and the whole thing is surprisingly detailed. From every hundred unfortunates punished in some form, we know that one was burned at the stake and ten to fifteen thrown in prison."

Clive is still not done, and Michael shuffles in his seat. "Yes, I know, pretty full on. But let's never forget, we're talking about a small part of the big picture back then, the south of France subject to serious social dislocation and trauma: nightmare stuff, and a serious imprint for generations."

"So, there you have it, absolute bloody turmoil for many more years, and in the humble opinions of The Frenchman and I; yes, events that would leave scars - Don's vibrations if you catch my drift - with some survivors fleeing to the north of Italy, and some to the north of France."

Michael is silent. He does get the picture, and it does get him thinking. "Could there be a weird connection to Don's dream after all?" He shakes his head. "Assuming there really was an actual dream, and not just another of Don's many stories."

Clive frowns and takes a deep breath, and stares at Michael. "Jesus. Are we talking intergenerational trauma here?"

| **45** |

Michael is happy Clive is not in the office today, and he has time to think without the theorizing of his old boss. There are two of Don's boxes to wade through. In the office back-room, he holds his breath, pulls those boxes aside and gathers up the notes. Back at his desk, he separates and sorts them, all entries from 1994 to 1996, Don moving between The Albert Hotel and the Central Victorian Goldfields.

- **March 1994/Goldfields, Vic**

Our first goal is the village, Gracie & me, Dad's inkbot on the map the only start we have. We'll stay one night & then back to The Albert for work. We reach the foothills late morning, pass old flour mills on riverbanks, some just shells, the bluestone bulky & black, the top levels floating on fog. More leftovers hug the higher hills, wrecked wooden home-steads, skinny brick chimneys often alone, silent sentinels on heaps of rubble, weeds waving to & fro.

Up the highway we check the map, these sheds & houses the village, a gully that straddles a creek, the highway over a wooden bridge, a servo with a cockeyed canopy & a kid at the pump with a green cricket cap, bumfluff for a beard, gives Gracie the once over, walks all the way around & smiles – Wow Buddy, she's fantastic, after a shaggin wagon meself. A bit of rust out back, but the powder blue is a bloody beauty!

We ask about the lay of the land & he looks up & down the highway, seems surprised, bites his lip & wonders why we'd be interested – To the west? Haha, you're jokin. Not much out there Buddy, just bush. Comes right up to the town, a bit too close for most around here.

I pull out the map & he raises his eyebrows – The old volcano? Ah, yep, looks OK on your map, but not sure about the road from here. S'pose you'd get a glimpse of it eventually, & you've got enough juice in the tank.

He pats Gracie's bonnet, tweaks his cap & looks up at the sky – & yeah, it is gettin late. Some pretty hairy tracks out there too Buddy, especially with you on your own. & hey. We've had some bloody big fires out there.

He's willing us to head east, not west, so waves a hand in that direction – The river's just over there Buddy. That's where I'd be goin if I was you, at least with what's left of to-day. Nice enough spot, lots of willows. Good campin. Bloody good sheep country further out, all cleared, rolling hills & granite.

We pull out & stop just down the highway, this meeting of potholed tracks, from nowhere & going nowhere, built by Newcomers, always something to dig up or milk dry, the highway the main street, a narrow strip of tar straight up the guts, over the bridge & north, the village cut in half, not that you'd notice. There's a bush side & a river side, like the servo kid said, more sheds than houses.

But there's always the churches, everywhere the churches, the Catholic of course, the Anglican & Primitive Methodist. & there's a Mechanics Institute, a lonely single room with a busted north wall. I light up a spliff, pick up a broken brick & see an errant tyre flying off a truck from way up the hill, bouncing over the fence, hitting the wall & leaving this hole. Other fences head this way & that, things needing edges, all about definition, Newcomers knowing what they own & where they sit in the overall scheme of things.

I still have the cards, think of one & see Mama back in Freo, sitting alone with black hair & shawl – This man, he wanders the snow, all alone, hooded head down, a long white beard, a lamp in his right hand, staff in the other. What we know sets us apart, but *oui*, you are on your own now.

Gracie's mudguard is cold on my bum, my pants wet. I blow clouds of smoke, not a soul around. But I'm never alone, a pounding in my head, the clatter of picks & shovels, steel on rock, 1000s toiling, shouting & cursing, all sorts drawn here, dreaming of gold like bees to honey, whiskers flecked with dust, the burning stench of gunpowder, the smell of sweat & a lingering summer, postcard plots to fight over, Blackfellas mostly gone, out of sight & out of mind.

Maybe that's Grandad drinking at the bar, this the last pub in the village, pulled down & turned to rubble, the bits and pieces used to build another bloke's dream down south, in sight of the old volcano but in the middle of nowhere, a conference centre, winery & restaurant surrounded by virgin bush. & I see the owner striding through his new restaurant in battered rubber boots & dirty singlet, the clash of cutlery on fine China plates, then the place in silence, the posh diners disgusted & long gone, the big room quiet, cobwebs that tremble, hot midday air that sticks in the throat, white linen with a layer of brown dust, wine glasses & crystal tumblers, a setting for gourmet ghosts. I see him standing outside, staring at the old volcano, another failed Newcomer dream, eyes emptied, the bush reclaiming its own.

My sandals raise dust from the village hotel rubble, my mind back in the here & now, wandering till I reach overgrown grass, the scattered sheds & houses all empty, falling down in their own time, street signs a rarity, some faded to naught, invisible subdivisions, the surveyor a man with high hopes, shaking hands & smiling, those signs leading nowhere, grassy roads of poisoned blackberries or just fenced off, locked gates & long skinny paddocks over underground reefs, the last mine a long time closed.

Back at the bridge, we turn off the highway to a gravel road, east to the river like the servo kid said. But Gracie pulls over on her own accord, shudders then stops on another bridge. I leave the door open, stand & stare, wooden rails low & rickety, crooked gaps & a raging creek, bullrushes waving in the slightest breeze, pencil stems & bumping heads full of fairy chatter.

Across the road lay a rough hewn trough, the length of Gracie & half as wide. I lean over, put my hand on the nearest wall, drag fingers along the edge, the stone cold & chipped, this water deep & still. I hear clip clop steps, newly shod shoes on a crushed rock road, the smell of sweat & leather, the approaching horse tired, thirsty & lathered in foam.

He's tall this bloke, saddle bags bulging, working garb dusty, wide hat stained, blue braces, baggy pants & black boots. He's a no fuss stockman & ringer, lean & a long way from home. A sleeping baby is cradled in the crook of his left arm, worn reins in his other hand. The horse snorts & slurps, big, big gulps, the reins tight around a brown weathered wrist.

I jump at a distant gunshot & the horse bolts, the baby slipping from the father's arm. I hear a splash, a bloodcurdling shout, his other arm wrenched away by the petrified horse, the pink bonneted baby left to gurgle & sink to the bottom. I gaze around, then down, the silence dreadful, the water still & black like glass. I see a tired face with lots of questions.

| 46 |

• **March 1994/Goldfields, Vic**

The sun is low & I leave Gracie by the river, shoulder my pack & hike along the bank, push through weeds, over tree stumps & rabbit holes, pitch my tent on the nearest bank. Willows are a maze of yellow, fine leaves & hideaway homes to tiny thornbills that flit & chatter. Hawthorns crowd the far side bank, branches long & arching. White cockatoos gorge on berries round & lipstick red, grasped in a single claw, yellow crests raised & heads cocked sideways. A single sentry stares from the highest tree, the look curious but critical. Suddenly there's a screech, the birds in full flight, air exploding, the rolling din up & down the valley. Finally, they settle in towering river gums, the loud calls of complaint, the raucous, bicker & jostle.

I browse my map & Michael's books, tribal lands & local mobs, the goldfields getting crowded, lines on maps with Newcomer names, me smoking, breathing in & blowing out. But still there's Mama's cards, the flowery diamond backs & pictures, memories of Mama fading but not gone. I hear that whisper, her dark straight hair – So, I see this young man, like you Donatien. Flowers surround him, a blanket draped over the shoulders, pure white tunic underneath, a snake for a belt. His right hand is skywards, the stick a wand, the other points to the earth. The sky is festooned with flowers. A small table sits in a field of lilies, on the table a cup, sword & pentangle. This is the material & the obvious, the here & now.

Newcomers are here with their upstream dams, wanting more & more, the river sucked dry, downstream just half full holes. & not many fish, not these days. This tree is a white bowled giant that's seen it all, ancient but alive, a gash in the trunk metres high, bark strip streamers from wide spread boughs.

& I hear Blackfellas chanting, the bark taken for a new canoe, but not right without permission, not right to cut trees or carelessly kill animals. The puddles deepen while I watch, the lapping of water & the smell of mud, before the rising salt, before the weeds, willows, & enough fish for all. Around the bend comes a single canoe, both ends bound with strips of bark, the middle braced open with sticks, the two blokes lean, one at the back with knees on the floor & paddle still. The other stands mid canoe, bolt upright & spear in hand. No need of clothes, all muscle & brawn, their church the earth & sky.

The canoe slides more than it moves, so low in the water, the standing bloke with spear raised, arm taught, muscles etched on arm & side, no need for ornaments, just ash & clay. Both are focused, stares fixed on a mirrored canvas of gum & wattle. I look away for one moment, then back, the deep black water just puddles again, the rakish black figures suddenly gone.

To Newcomers, no one lives here, not really, the canoes the worst they've seen, primitive, frugal & spare. The future is here with a bang, the smallpox outbreaks, a flu epidemic, the guardian spirits not happy with the way of things & Newcomers moving quickly to grab the best land. There's fighting, hunting grounds gone, downcast eyes, Blackfellas with nowhere to go & problems with mobs nextdoor.

| 47 |

• **August 1995/The Albert, Melbourne Bayside**

Been here at The Albert for over a year, coming & going. Yeah Siss, that's me all over, this old pub a little piece of Freo, only on the other side of the country, putting some cash together, get my life on some sort of track, maybe this time actually heading somewhere. It's something about Grandad, the few bits that Dad told me, & Michael, me taking a different tack to sort stuff out, where I'm from & who I am, Grandad living within sight of some old volcano before heading west to Kalgoorlie way. Yeah Siss, I know what you think of Dad, & I could never talk to you about that, not in a month of Sundays.

& I'm the first to admit nothing is certain, me now with a new bunch of stories I seem to already know, about the village, memories that linger, about thousands struggling to make a living, the clatter of picks & shovels that bang in my head, the acrid smell of gunpowder, the visions of a Grandad I never knew, grimy faced and whiskers flecked with dust. & then there's the residue of an idea that started with Kelvin, me only 18 but on the edge of something. But it's not Kelvin's country down on that river. Don't think he's ever seen a canoe, but he knew about ash & clay.

The hotel room's hazy, the curtains hanging heavy, the movement slight, my smoke in layers below the ceiling, the plaster rose a broken circle, a lightshade fringe that trembles. My eyes fall on the table, my bulging beat up satchel with the busted zip, the plastic kettle & cup, the lamp on the floor my guardian angel. & there's Mama's cards, one face up & on its own, now between my finger & thumb.

Mama looks puzzled, fiddles with the tortoiseshell combe in her hair – She's the real angel, *oui*, tall like your lamp, golden hair, long dress all white. You see the triangle on her chest, those red wings wide. See how she pours water from one chalice to another? Her left foot is on the stones Donatien, the other in the pond, the mountains far away.

I see it now, the whole thing a balancing act. But I'm anxious to learn, digging deep, looking for a path. One thing for sure, there's no escaping the stories. They follow me around with nowhere safe.

Again I hear sobbing down The Albert hallway, young girls in nightgowns, shadows outside my room, a fleeting blackout of the gap under the door, the gaping keyhole darkened for a second. The passage floor squeaks, someone outside. They hesitate then shuffle on. But I know from Andreas there's no other guests, & it's far too early for Andreas. Snoopy patrons from downstairs? Maybe more than one, lost in this newest wing, another seeker of solitude like me, another escapee.

But then they're gone, no shadow, the light back in the old keyhole.

• September 1995/The Albert, Melbourne Bayside

It's another trip north for me & Gracie, the map laid out yet again on the high iron bed, this inkblot the village & the goldfields, then finally west, past the Water Bailiff's, the old coach road our only option, until we see the old volcano to the south. Yeah Siss, I know, I may get nothing out of this at all. But bet you're happy I've got a plan for once.

& yet the old doubts are still there, that servo kid, the bumfluff & cricket cap that doesn't quite fit – Going west from here? Well, best of bloody luck Buddy, guess you know what you're doin. All the way out there just to get a glimpse of some old volcano. You take care of that wagon Buddy.

| **48** |

West from the highway we pass the Mechanics Institute, churches & pull over. I throw open the door, step out & sniff the air, the valley loaded with wood smoke from sparsely scattered chimney stacks. The coach stables are empty, rickety but intact, the hitching rails weathered, rough to the touch, wooden roosts for magpie carols.

Like the servo kid says, it's a border of sorts, the morning sun behind us, the Water Bailiff's cottage where it should be, perched on the edge of a flat earth, the place long empty, walls on a lean, the gate shut & padlocked. I stand & stare, the top rail rusted, my fingertips orange. There's a chook shed fallen down, weeds in the gutter of a holey iron roof, the ground covered in dried chicken shit, the cottage walls once white.

There's the faint crow of a rooster & a faded face in a broken window. He's blind & lonely, rides a donkey to church on Sunday. I smell bleach as plain as day, his chooks like family, 7 Chinese silkies each one a dazzling white, spoilt rotten & washed in the kitchen sink. He gets a lift to the city & shows his prize babies each year.

But now there's just me, all that gone, no more gold, no Bailiff & no chooks, no honest farming folk, behind the cottage the water channel, the crooked posts & the barbwire busted, tangled thickets of blackberry & gorse, nasty stuff & razor sharp.

We stop at the water channel crossing, my footsteps ringing on the cattle grate pipes, the rush of water underneath, through the sluice, all gurgle & swish. I breathe in the eucalyptus & the smell of damp earth, a pair of ducks wondering why I'm here. There's the twitter of birds, the blue flash of wrens with tails held high, a dance on top of channel walls. Moss is Irish green, mauve flowers like tiny flags, the channel embankment falling west into the bush on both sides of the old coach road. Gracie's tyres rumble over grate & channel. The exhaust rattles, our way straight ahead & into the bush, the old coach road a track, suddenly narrow & scrub brushing my shirtsleeve, no prying eyes, no questions from here on in. I stare at the map on the passenger's seat.

• September 1995/Goldfields, Vic

Stands of pines straddle the road just here, tall, dark & brooding, toadstools off to the side, orange capped with white spots, elfin beacons in shifting shadows, a carpet of needles, the smell of dust & turpentine, the silence deafening. I turn the key, Gracie rolling but full of complaints, the road rough & uneven. I'm thinking the more holes & bumps the better.

There's rocks on the road from way up the hill, just here a fallen tree. I steer Gracie aside, push & pull until the branches are clear, stand & brush the dirt from my shirt & strides, pick a stone from my sandals. The air's a heady combo, leaves alive & dead, rocky drains full of broken branches & dirt.

Here's a tee intersection, a fire tower in ruins, the warm air quiet & restful. But I hear wild winds of days gone by, see the fallen trunks & busted branches. I crush leaves between my fingers, the scent minty & camphorous. I yawn, take a swig from my water bottle & roll a spliff, easy to get lost, the bush so thick, the sounds soft. Secret trackside clearings are bathed in wells of light, clumps of heath in pink & white. But I've wandered again, Gracie waiting back there on the road, her bonnet patchy through the trees, old paths everywhere, on shale & rock. I follow the faintest tyre tracks to a ring of rough barked gums, the sweet smell of honey, a humming in my ears, the buzz & whirl of bees, sunlit wings like silver. In the centre are doll house boxes, white, stacked all higgeldy piggeldy.

Away from the clearing I peer up into the highest canopy, yellow box stands, tall & straight, the rustle of leaves. There's something about the light, the bush so different, the stories different, the light homogenous, an endless sea of filtered grey, the last spray of wattle, the perfume pungent, no Peru or France.

Gracie hits a rock & I slow, the shadows longer, a machine off to the side & almost hidden. We stop & I stare, this lurking, brooding beast asleep in its lair, a rusted menace ready to pounce in days gone by, suddenly awake & hard at work, the rain all gone, a new paint job, red & roaring, belching black smoke, gouging & pushing, shifting dirt from here to there, wild hills reshaped, the old coach road a fire track, drains & culverts to keep clear, the dozer driver fat with a bad cough, hairy arms yanking this way & that. He's hunched over the wheel, a soggy smoke in the corner of his mouth, belly between his knees & bum crack above baggy blue shorts. There's the roar & crash, the crunch of rock.

The old coach road lay straight ahead, tough going, steering Gracie downhill, the tyres in deep gouges, then planting the foot uphill. Cuttings are steep & awkward, wrought by Newcomers, the pick, the shovel, horse & cart. High quartz reefs with stark white bluffs, broken pieces tumbling down to the old coach road.

I turn off the engine & listen, Gracie hot, creaking & finally still, a distant rumble from years long gone, the collective clatter of coaches, speeding, urgent, onwards & northwards. There's the clank of steel on rock, the shouts, the yelling & cursing, the crack of a whip, flying stones like missiles, then broken & spent, white quartz chunks like packing box styrene. But this is it for me & Gracie, the old coach road turning north.

We head south, the contours falling to the old volcano, the shadows long at this crossing of paths, a good place to camp, this a gathering of half walls, holes & mounds, a land of leftover ghosts, me in a tent on the ground by Gracie, a handful of beans & nuts enough. I huddle down & lay still, my nose frozen. Cold air seeps between me & the bag whenever I turn, my head full of whispers, the shuffle of freezing feet, the sometimes snow in Spring, the ridges of rock, eyes downcast, whiskered faces weathered, worried & furrowed.

In the morning I'm up with the sun, stomping feet & clapping hands to get warm. The footings were once houses of stone, now tumbled down, another reef underfoot, untended apple & mulberries wild, broken walls & paths, my sandals slipping on crushed rock, gravel between my toes, pushing past a rosemary bush, the smell of camphor & lemon. But there's a vibe here I just don't like, arsenic that seeps through this ancient ground, these hills all tailings, tracks among secret shafts & shifted rock, the rambling bush engulfing & grey.

So, this track is dead south, away from the old coach road, scrub closing in, branches that bang & thump, poor Gracie copping a beating, for who knows how long, a noise jolting me from my daydreams, another branch stuck in the wheel. I jump out, pull it clear, my map & compass on the hot bonnet. Now I'm certain, this track too turning, rising westward up ahead & parallel to the old coach road, our way south if we'll ever see the old volcano. But there'll be no more driving, this a goat track south, overgrown & easily missed.

| 49 |

The track is definitely heading south, but can't see how far from up here, just a forever rolling blanket of bush. The contours are right, the old volcano out there, but how far will this track actually take me? I leave Gracie half hid, but don't know why I bother. Even the old coach road's rarely used, the unseen beekeeper, the dozer driver long gone, me & Gracie the only idiots here, according to the servo kid. I open the back & pull my pack from all the junk, load up the tent, my precious satchel & latest scribbles, Michael's books, some food & water. I know what Siss would say – You bet Brother. Up to your old freakin tricks, no idea where you're going, or why the hell you're going there.

Yeah, I know Siss, but the track does go somewhere, for 3 hours, me winding & pushing through scrub until one last bend, a tall brick chimney above all else, a house, the east wall a red brick gable. So, there you go Siss, a bloody house, way out here. A chimney & stone hearth, a creeper in the cracks with purple buds like beacons.

And there's jonquils here, clumps of the things, yellow & white, the grass green but grazed short by wombats & roos. The verandah's narrow & barely head high, a porch all dirt, the single window a small opening, a stone step up to a gaping doorway. I peer inside, the gloom & dust, some floor-boards intact, rocks in the fireplace, the back wall planks full of gaps. I turn to the door jamb, jagged holes where the hinges once were, the timber rough & torn, the door ripped off & dumped down the gully in past wild weather.

Under the verandah I stub my toe on a rock, the hard dirt dusty & dry. I light up, the smoke pierced by sunlit shafts through holes in the iron overhead. I gaze up & down the front wall, rough sawn slabs, weathered grey, the west end propped up by an ancient mulberry, half dead, half alive, twisted, furrowed & bent.

• September 1995/Goldfields, Vic

Behind the house is much higher ground, different ground, the goat track winding past the house, along the west wall & up the hill, the bush thinner, the scrub scattered until I stand on a rocky spur. I pull out the map & check the contours, nothing between the old volcano & me. I stare south from beside the upturned roots of a giant that's fallen, the trunk as wide as I am tall, the stripped crown laying 20m down the hill & into the bush, the horizon 10km off & the old goat track overgrown until completely gone. Shit, my stomach is churning. I should see the old volcano from here.

But no, it's not where it should be, the horizon blurred by a bank of cloud. I just don't see it, not really, but I want to see it, think I see it, the hint of a truncated mantle, a memory, the old doubts back, me out here in the middle of nowhere, another waste of time like France. How much do I really know? Only what Dad says, & Michael's books, me making up the rest, olden days, tough times, Grandad's whereabouts, grabbing any work he can. Well, that's a bucket more than I knew about France I suppose.

The gums up here are different, white bowled giants, drenched pink in latish sun, strips of bark that hang like streamers, the spur running from east to west. One last look south, & time for camp, crawling in my tent & sleeping bag, leaving the end open, pull off a glove & reach outside, one hand on the ground, the stones, rough & uneven, smoking, head spinning in the darkness, Siss never far away, the clunk of her bracelet as she joins me in a smoke − Brother. Another wild freakin goose chase! Don't you be expecting too much.

Clouds of dope are trapped in the ridge of the tent, the dawn taking its time, waves of raindrops a patter above, my tongue furry from too many spliffs. I cough, half asleep, half awake. It feels like morning, but it's still dark, a distant moan & sorry business, Blackfellas hiding all around. There's trouble up north past the old coach road, the shouts & the wailing, women & children, 40 killed, the bodies cut up & burned.

When anything's missing, the whole mob's guilty. Heads shake in high places, government officials winge & complain. But there's better ways to deal with thieving Blackfellas, less obvious ways & arsenic a good messenger. They're eating damper laced with the stuff, kids rolling in dirt, swollen bellies, skinny legs thrashing. Again, burn the bodies, can't be recognized, frantic eyes looking this way & that, Blackfella souls lost & confused, rising from smoke with nowhere to go. Another mob is poisoned, this mob a big one. & now it's too late, not many left, Blackfellas refusing Newcomers' bread or milk, staying hungry, starvation better than getting poisoned & burned.

I roll out from the tent at god knows what hour, sleeping bag soaked by morning & smelling like sour bread, an open sky of washed grey, no idea what's happening, see Grandad's face, a wide brim hiding narrow eyes. I turn & follow the trunk of this fallen giant south, down the hill & across the bush to the horizon, & finally the truncated form of the old volcano. Grandad's Mount, within reach of the village & finally a story that means something. I see Siss disgusted, shakes her head & quaffs another drink.

• December 1995/Goldfields, Vic

Now I'm coming & going, The Albert one day, up here on the spur the next, plenty of time to think, away from the city, the distractions & the unimportant. The air's thick, the scent of gums like honey, the flowers in bunches, the buzz of bees, big trunks pink & white, ribbons of bark that rustle in warm north winds. These white bowled giants are special, wrought from solid rock, gnarly roots embedded tentacles, always searching, the seasons hot to freezing cold. Don't know why they're way up here, real old, from earlier times, ants gnawing at pained hearts, dark & dangerous, memories of mayhem & murder, twisted broken branches all about. They crack & fall with no warning, a crash no one hears on the stillest of days, widow makers, ancient justice, bent boughs arching & angry.

| 50 |

• **January 1996/Goldfields, Vic**

The house is perched down the hill from the spur, this shallow cut off drain behind, pick & shovel, testament to other times. & I know how wild it gets, see & smell the changing seasons, hear the spring rain on the roof, & in winter the clatter from cold sheets of hail, see the scours in the dirt, a river of water from up the hill, over this scrape of a drain to gurgle through the gaps in the back wall, across the floor & through the doorless opening, across the step & down the gully.

But Siss, she looks around – Get a grip Brother. So you've struck it lucky & seen your freakin mountain. But really, you're going to live where?

Yeah, I get it, I do, but I've done it before. Less work than Freo, that's for sure, weathered wallboards grey, rough & hand hewn, some just hanging, the nails rusted, some broken or bent, the west wall rickety at best, the giant mulberry timeless, desperate, one branch about to topple & take the house with it. Inside's full of cobwebs, swallows in the open window space & out the doorway. I see glimpses of sky through the roof, drag Dad's tools up from Gracie, prop up bricks, block holes & gaps with broken boards from the gully below. Drafts tug at the tarp, & I worry at my latest scribbles being blown to the 4 winds.

There are jobs for another day, the darkness & spliff making me think, the Freo warehouse, Maricielo, me wasting her time while I'm sorting things out, her so small in that big club chair, the little black dress, her reflection in the glass, windows & door, the ferns & fountain in the courtyard outside. In the end she was different, serious, that wild side gone, me wondering what to do & Robbo shaking his head.

I stare out from under the verandah & across at the sky, the last shafts of light through patches of grey, the wind dying with the weakening sun. White flashes are wings, oddly out of synch, the screech & bark, cockatoos & corellas heading home from ploughed western plains. Summer's the worst time, so the servo kid says – Fires come from nowhere Buddy, so watch yourself out there, keep your wits about ya.

Out front I roll another spliff & sniff the air, see smoke, the servo kid not born yet. There's a wind change from north to west & the house shudders. I see the door blown open, ripped off its hinges, the bush ablaze like a runaway train to the old coach road & village, fierce fires on too many fronts, furious flames & sparks that spit, village faces full of fear, wide eyed women & kids in the river, most the men away. Next it's jumped the river, good sheep country, thousands burnt, stinking piles in paddock corners, the pathetic bleat of the many maimed.

At night I stare back at the house, somehow spared, more

black than the bush. I poke at campfire coals, eyes heavy, count trunks like sheep, the bark scarred from those horrors past, me just a kid, at the other side of the country, Mama with her own stories of fire & retribution, of Medieval dragons, their burning breath, her black shawl & lavender soap. Then we're alone Siss, just you & me, a rainy day & Mama's funeral.

I'm due back at The Albert tonight, push my gear in the corner, adjust the tarp, stack Dad's tools against the wall & grab some food. Down at the junction I pull branches from Gracie's bonnet, think of the kid at the servo. He'd love to get his hands on her & I can see Siss' face, disgusted at the thought of wasting good money on a beat up bomb like Gracie – I'll tell you what Brother, that rustbucket's a freakin deathtrap.

• July 1996/Goldfields, Vic

So this is it, lugging the last of my stuff from The Albert to here, hard going at first & freezing cold, 3 hours from Gracie to the house, the soles of my sandals wearing thin, the canvas pack heavy, Michael's books, my satchel & the latest scribbles. One more trip from Gracie to the house, the dope, the beans & porridge. I flop in front of the verandah among newly sprouted jonquils. Afternoon mist merges with the grey box canopy, rough dark trunks blurred & barely visible, silent, shrouded sentinels, the front door still missing, my stuff a pile in a corner by the fireplace, but not too close, the tarp over the lot.

Sleep won't come, me tossing & turning, the whole place creaking & no one there. I throw on a jacket & wander out the open doorway, stare along the wallboards & verandah posts, the wood rough sawn.

There's a banging in the back of my mind, a bloke outside with a hammer, then an adze, a stack of hand hewn boards on the ground, a good place for a house he growls. This bloke's bad tempered, a loner & mostly drunk, long coat & a lump on his back, his leather hat lopsided. With the house built, he's gone for weeks, returns from down past Grandad's Mount. He staggers behind a brown bullock with whip in hand, leads Chinese hopefuls from South Australia to here, then to village goldfields, the long trek avoiding a tax the Chinamen can't afford. He dies of lockjaw alone in the village, bones buried in the paupers' corner. The Chinamen are harassed, hounded, accused of foul play, claim jumping & molesting white women, then bashed with picks & shovels.

The wind wanders the old coach road, the guarded whispers Cantonese, 5 dead but refused a burial, their bodies dragged to the house on makeshift stretchers, jonquils planted for good luck. I drift down the gully, slide in the gravel, an ancient wild apple the lone remnant of a market garden. I find my front door way down here, leave it for later, scrap around among the rubbish. There's a rusted, wheeled contraption a long way from the paddock it ripped & cleared, the gully riddled with blackberry & bits of iron, busted hinges, cans & bottles, a handful of round coins with square holes.

Fenceposts lean like drunken sailors, hand carved holes

gaping, empty, the wire long gone, on my side comfort in the familiar, all about ownership, more good luck jonquils, the bush air heady, 5 graves just piles of rock, all quiet & unadorned. On the other side is the bush, the unattainable, the impossible to understand & the unwanted, a foreign land best kept at arm's length, those grey trunks like sad blokes in pyjamas, always outside looking in, eyes narrow, uncertain, pigtails with pale faces skywards. They pine for home & family, wonder where their fortunes lie, this land so vast, so big, something they'll never fathom. The fortunate ones leave, sew gold sovereigns in deep pockets for safe keeping, then drown at sea, their boats flimsy & the gold like lead.

But they're here to do their fathers proud & I hear a sage from over the sea – When a father is alive, we must look at the inclination of the father's will. Once dead, we must look at his son's conduct. If the son does not alter from the way of his father, only then can he be called his father's son.

| 51 |

With nightfall I'm out front of the house, my breath a frosty cloud, the eucalypt bush all camphor & cut mint, the hills awash with mist. There's the slightest rustle of leaves, no moon, the blackness engulfing, the cold thick like soup. I can't see my hand in front of my face, until I look up & stare, my spread hand a Blackfella cave painting, the scattered canopy of unknown worlds, The Dark Emu & Warrior. It's way past Kelvin's bedtime.

Then later there's the moon, a giant yellow orb raised above rolling hills, the densest night replaced with light, the bush a blanket silver & black. I'm drifting, away from the house but no chance of tripping or falling down a hole, no danger of rambling off lost to die of cold. & I see things, always do, shadows through time, hear footsteps, scurries, squeaks and rustles, scales that scrape in the deepest holes, a wallaby scratting at the chimney, the grunt & roar of a wayward koala.

Inside later, the fire crackles, the front door finally back on its hinges, me sitting, fiddling with the cards. & I wonder. Is it really about Grandad's Mount? Maybe just seeing it is enough. OK, I hear you Siss, me paranoid, scared of finishing anything, awake all hours, smoking too much, this dope the seed of more crazy stories.

Dad would never say as much, but has no time for stories either. Definitely no time for the cards, Mama's poison he says. But he's always happy when I turn up, dropping by after work & now whenever I can manage. He's always worked hard, makes the best of everything but with something to prove. Me? Still got the cards in my pocket & yeah, still know them by heart. This one's a swirling lake, a pair of dogs under a yellow moon, one wild & one not. The sky's dark & starry, a lobster crawling from the water & a winding path to far off mountains. If only I can balance the past with the present, the answer inside, not outside.

I stare at the card, this man in the moon, the ancient face furrowed, this other world that's always been there, all about sorting stuff, of trials, journeys & evolution, 65 thousand years & longer, the Great Spirit making mountains, valleys from rock, rivers, trees & desert. Animals come from the water, then the first Blackfellas & spirits down deep wherever we walk.

In the morning I climb up to the spur, stand by the fallen giant, the roots an upturned spiderweb, stare south over bush that rolls down from the spur, all quiet. Grandad's Mount is as clear as day, to the east a forest thick, to the west a sadness, sorry business a shadow over parched plains.

Special places. What's imagined & what's not. I'm thinking Peru, the power of place at the heart of things, a feeling here & there, a foreign vibe, being short of breath or tingling feet, intersecting paths, some friendly & others not, getting sick for no reason, dormant cancers suddenly aggressive, aching bones, arthritis, elbows inflamed, the pain unbearable, inherent memories that lay dormant in footprints for 1000s of years.

| 52 |

• **September 1996/ Goldfields, Vic**

Up on the spur I take in a spliff, the late mist low, clammy
& cold, jacket collar turned up, beanie pulled down, llama
wool warm & soft. My eyes drift south, Grandad's Mount
afloat a cottonwool sea, a single wisp of cloud from that
conical peak. Dusk rolls in, white noise too, a rattle & rumble
from the old coach road.

In the morning I tackle the house, the front door & step,
the cut off drain & old stone well, water from the spring,
tweak the well inlet & clear the overflow down to the gully
& creek bed. Done for the day, I push at the door to fetch my
latest scribbles, all about keeping stuff dry & my writing safe.

Inside I poke around this single room & remember the
servo kid, the seed sown – & hey. We've had some bloody big
fires out there.

So, I worry, don't I Siss? Smell smoke. I see black on the
rafters, above the hearth too, & a floorboard badly burnt. I
see one dark night, years ago in the dead of winter, a wiry
bloke with a hump back, the night bitter, an empty whisky

bottle on its side, the house frame dry as chips, gritty wood spitting sparks from a hearth of stone.

Suddenly the house seems claustrophobic & dangerous, a faulty fireplace & flue, the danger of being burned alive as I kick & scream, all tangled up in my sleeping bag, the door jamb stuck & the door shut, the window too small & too high to climb out. I dread the thought of losing my scribbles, stand at the window looking out, gasping for air, the breeze on my face, elbows on the splintered sill.

Out front, it's bitterly cold & all still, me finally breathing easy, surrounded by good luck jonquils, the perfume heady, sweet, the house behind me, the creaks & shadows, the first wind rattling the iron roof & rolling in waves across black bush hills. I turn on my side & prop on my elbow, the sleeping bag pulled up under my armpits, the bush so silent, the wind gone with the dead of night.

Cold seeps from rocky ground, the sky icy. I tug at my beanie warm on my ears, pick at a can of beans, drawn to the campfire like a moth to a flame. I fiddle with my satchel with the busted zip, shiver & shake, shuffle sheets of paper, another spliff & scribble, the night full of half sleeps & dreams. I wake with a start, the fire smouldering, one sheet of scribbles smoking, in the coals where it fell, my satchel safe on the ground. I poke at the fire, need to get a handle on things, clean up my act, no more dope. Just like that. Without my scribbles, I've nothing.

| 53 |

I've been putting this off, my head clear, a trip for stores & materials. Nothing much at the village, so no excuses. There's a town down south near Grandad's Mount. I pack Michael's books & my satchel, hike down to Gracie in the dark, hate the thought of questions, leaving early to beat the farmers, the teachers & kids dropped off at school.

Gracie takes a bit to start, sitting out there in the middle of nowhere. She feels every bump as we turn back to the intersection nearer to the old coach road. This time we head west, away from the village, the bush finally fading to bare paddocks, long straight fences & lonely ring barked trunks. We turn south towards the town, find the main street deserted & kill some time down by the lake. I leave Gracie by the boat shed, sit on the railing & watch the mist on the water. It's odd, thinking of Mama, the fog like smoke & the wooden jetty legless, aglow & on fire with the first hint of sun.

I sit facing the water, an approaching multi coloured fleet, ducks, geese & coots. They quack & honk expecting food, but my head's somewhere else not far away, Grandad's Mount northeast of here. I wonder why I've been hesitant, if the view from up on the spur was somehow enough, if the house & goldfields are more relevant to the stories that crowd my head.

& I see Siss larger than life, always with the answers, those lips & nails red & freshly painted. She shakes her head – Well Brother, you're freakin well here, for whatever the reason, so maybe you should at least take a look.

Firstly it's the town, finally awake, & I turn back into the main street at the hilltop hotel, the tall pointed tower another grand statement, the mandatory horse trough, this one full of weeds. I park & wander, past the town hall, another monument to another time, another El Dorado come & gone, the hill streets cold & windy, my jacket collar turned up, the smells from the bakery taking me back to Mama's kitchen, early days, a familiar waft of lavender from a craft shop trestle table, the wide pavements otherwise empty & bleak.

This bloke at the wreckers wants to chat, stocky build, Irish lilt & steel capped gumboots, with iron sheet seconds & timber going cheap. He frowns, wants to know what I'm doing out there in the bush by myself, where I've been & where I'm going. But I'm weary of that before he even starts, the tailgate down, Gracie waiting & empty for the first time in years. Siss would be disgusted, filling Gracie with more junk, iron in the back, the sheets already rusty. But they'll do the job Siss, don't you worry. Next, it's a bag of nails & second hand boards. I pick up food in the health shop, drive slowly, rattle & scrape complaints from the back, no traffic on the tracks I take.

I see Grandad's Mount for real from a mile off, pull over & gaze, edgy as I approach the last turnoff, chest tight, butter-flies in the pit of my stomach, the spectre a conical profile. But it's different from this angle, like a lost memory I struggle to recall, way above the rolling plains & pastures, to the north the bush, a rolling grey horizon, the old coach road, spur & house unseen.

It's an odd feeling, me really here, Gracie needing encour-agement on the steeper slopes, my foot down, the road wind-ing, a bend near the top, plantation pines around the crown, the foreign foliage dark & sombre. I think of Grandad's day, Blackfellas & Newcomers, tough times when nothing comes for free, him here somewhere, then heading west to the great unknown. The thing is, I don't know much at all, Michael's books, Dad's map with an inkblot in the middle.

With school finally done, I saw him now & then. But it's like he didn't want to talk, not interested in the old days. But he was there for me I suppose. Early times? Siss & me just kids. Then all of a sudden, he's gone. May as well have disappeared into thin air as far as Siss is concerned – You freakin bet Brother, along with all his church hangers on & his own life kept secret, like he was ashamed or something. & so he freakin should be, the way we were treated.

I pull Gracie off the road again when closer, stop & stare up at the volcano cone, whispered tales from way back, a column of smoke, fire belching from the top, the stink of sulphur, a threatening place, a warning of what's to come. Same old same old, stories on stories. There's just no escape, the vibes everywhere I turn. How much do I know & how much is in my head?

Late afternoon & I'm here, in the heart of it, the towering trees an odd montage that just doesn't belong, the wide sweeping boughs, the still bare poplars, round concrete picnic tables and tottering pedestal stools. Random piles of pine cones cast long shadows, the grass mowed short by roaming roos.

I leave Gracie at the crater wall, no townsfolk or tourists, the tables & toilet block deserted. There'll be tents & camper vans in summer but now the ground's still cold, no birds & not a breath of wind. & yet there's a rustle of dried leaves that cling to desolate oaks, the earth dank, the lingering smell of rotting leaves, the pine needles, the ground a tapestry of red, yellow & brown, a promise of rain that hangs in the air & fills my nostrils.

My tent's tied to Gracie's bumper & the nearest tree, me settled on the grass in the gloom, a lone black beetle on the ground, then ambling across my sandal strap. It's like I'm waiting, here in the guts of Grandad's Mount. Until I crawl out, stand & head up to the lookout, the last of the sun, on an ancient path that rises. I stop, prop for a moment, peer over my shoulder, inside the crater dark. There's a residue like vibration, the pungent power of place, the fragrance of a flower at the end of its life or something more foreboding, a dreaming of grief or pain, a sorry business not far away, extreme longing or regret, a load of stuff that won't go away.

From the edge of the rim I stare out, away to the north, imagine the distant bush, the old coach road & house I now call home, then behind me again. A shadow rises inside the crater, voices too, soft at first then urgent, a Blackfella hunting party. They sit on their haunches across the rim, spears to the sky, one pointing out & away, eyes narrowed, westward to a setting sun, the cleared plains, the ring barked stumps once white bowled giants on an ancient tended parkland.

Black faces turn to each other, shaking shaggy heads, pointing & handwaving, a strip of sun under a bank of clouds. They wonder about these Newcomers from the south, who they are & where they're going. But it's all too late. I listen, a rumbling from over the horizon, & maybe a howl, the hunting party suddenly gone. I see times that change, the barb wire fences new, hedges all prickle & spikes, the sun sinking & ominous.

A flat horizon is yellow & pink, with finally the hint of a breeze & the smell of rain, the last hurrah of a dying sun, the upward afterglow from blacktop banks of cloud, a flash of lightning & a distant rumble. But then I see it, or think I do, at the foot of Grandad's Mount, a red brick wall, almost hid by stands of cypress, what's left of the Mission, built for protection, handouts of flour, salt & sugar. There's food if you stay inside the precious fences, behave like Newcomers. Thou shall not steal.

I think of Grandad, tough going, communities best sorted like an English village, civilised & modern. But these Black-fellas, they never stay in one place, can't be relied on for anything, don't abide by the good book rules, wander & go walkabout for days. They don't write a thing, use tracks that can't be seen, no shoes & throwing good clothes away. Government men & Mission Protectors ensure a proper education, cultural absorption the simple solution. Get them on board as kids, the earlier the better, then maybe there's a chance of sorting them out, giving these Blackfellas half a chance.

Surrounding farms are large, lonely places, Newcomers longing for home, graziers & shepherds taking Blackfella women, guns a good persuader. From the lookout I'm back in the crater, now inky black, my shuffling sandaled feet like foreign echoes, the pitter patter of raindrops on dirt, the rush of pine needles. I tug at the tent zip & crawl inside, can't sleep with the roar of wind, the onslaught of hail, the crash & clatter.

The downpour stops as quick as it started. Silence. I drag myself back outside to a rustle of branches, rhythmic clicks & a wail of voices from the heart of the clearing, the crater shadows far too dark. There's an almighty sizzle, a crack, the flash of lightning, all floodlit, talking sticks & Blackfellas dancing, white stripe flashes on faces, chests, arms & legs. They dance in lines, a leafy branch in every hand, bodies stomping, swaying, all in a row, then a semicircle.

But I don't know what's happening, the entire group collapsed, eyes closed, bodies a tangle, heads buried in clumps of leaves, all still, a lifeless hill heaped in the centre of the crater. There's a long silence, then a shout that makes me jump, the human lump splitting apart & all on their feet, branches waved high & trembling. I gaze this way & that, no stars, no moon, not way down here. & then I get it, all the dead now reborn.

Later I'm sleeping, or trying to, unzip & poke my head out, the sky now clear & cold, the insistent dripping from surrounding branches, a shooting star across the crater, then gone behind the western rim. I wish it would go back to where it came. I pack Michael's books in the dark, my cards & satchel of scribbles, leave at sunrise. It's back to the house, except I've something else to see.

| **54** |

From the Mission turnoff it's a short walk to the burying ground in the shadow of Grandad's Mount. The track's uneven, overgrown, the gate crooked & scraping the ground. It creaks when I push it open, stop & gaze around, the surrounding hills bare, rows of slow motion sheep with lowered heads.

The first job for the surveyor is to make a place for the dead, in the right place he says. No one asks these Blackfellas anything, the Surveyor dying without warning & the first to be buried, his body here under the closest headstone. Next lay the Mission Protector, the Caretaker & Constable. The Cook is last, the ryegrass stubble & air damp from last night's rain, the sky washed blue & clear.

An invisible path leads way up back to Blackfella bones on neglected plots. & there's been fire, like it follows me about, the history purged like fire does, nothing to see here, the small wooden crosses & records all gone, Newcomers' are frantic to save the fence & the redgum posts still here.

I sit between graves, stubble waving in the breeze, sniff damp dirt & pick grass seeds from between my toes. There's just no peace in a place that's foreign, Blackfella mobs chucked together, Jaara, Wergaia, Wadi Wadi & Yorta. I see them all, Blackfella faces, names in my head that can't be said, like they never existed in the first place.

Bodies should buried in one piece, holding the spirit after death, a proper funeral in a proper place, this country not right, not home. & a body needs brothers, sisters, uncles & aunties, all kin important, here, by the body with special gifts, shade from summer sun, the right respect & ritual for days. If not, there'll be trouble, bad stuff for those left behind.

But this is the modern world, the Newcomers' world. There's a line of women, kids, Blackfellas walking slow, heads low like those sheep on the hill, the Mission church service compulsory. At best they're all children, understanding nothing, so the Protector says.

There's Newcomer rules to follow, Blackfellas herded here by the fence, standing around & looking lost, this hole in the ground, yellow clay in a pile, a Newcomer in a black suit, silver beard & high hat. He clears his throat, clutches his book in one hand out front, raises the other & points to the sky, thin lips, Newcomer words, the body in its open box, face frail & coffee coloured, eyes closed, grey hair bound, a stiff white dress, full length with scalloped neck, hammer raised & box nailed shut, no gifts for her journey.

Grandad's Mount sees it all, hears it all & remembers it all, the sobs, the wails, the gnashing of teeth, fewer family or friends, the beating of arms & skinny legs, the bruises &

bleeding, the cuts a comfort, the pain gone when the blood dries.

Another woman is Yorta, no family, no warriors of neighbouring mobs, no mourners, no charcoal or clay. Another lonely death, a fearful death, a lost spirit in a foreign land, her hole dug by an Irish kid, coffins in short supply. Forgotten bodies lay in sunken, shallow holes, baking bones barely buried.

There's wailing from a long way off, across cleared pastures, the rolling hills northwards, past the bush, way past the house & the old coach road.

From the burying ground it's the next paddock, the scattered broken bricks, what's left of the Mission proper, the stands of cypress, the battered branches busted from past raging winds. The sun appears above Grandad's Mount, the shade suddenly gone, a red brick wall among the cypress, the old church a single room, squarish, the gable high, the crooked iron cross making my stomach churn. Sad faces are all in a row, eyes blank, women & kids, collected up & covered in blankets, pushed & prodded, can't be seen naked, all marched here to Sunday sermon.

A couple stand at the end but slightly apart, floating in & out of focus, the bloke with a rifle barrel held tight, upright with wooden stock on the ground. He's head & shoulders above the rest, wide brimmed hat pulled down, eyes half hid until he lifts his head & returns my stare. My heart jumps, butterflies in my stomach, but I don't understand. It's Dad, a woollen suit, drab & grey, the jacket & pants baggy, muddy boots, a woman by his side, short, the face dark, eyes glazed, stiff white dress, long sleeves and hem, the collar high. Her feet are bare.

There's not much left of the Protector's homestead, the broken bricks, the timber taken & turned into barns, sheds, & fences for miles around. The rest of the settlement is half walls & rubble, what's left of cottages, those of the Manager, the Constable & Cook just here, the Overseer & Blacksmith at the end.

The sun's on my back & I turn & stare, high above, Grandad's Mount against a clear blue sky, the sun rising each & every day, the land all cleared, game hunted & chased away. Paddocks are subdivided, cut up by wire, posts & hedges, thorn & prickle, Blackfellas squeezed into even smaller pockets farther away. Land is money. & now there's no work, Government rations needed, priorities clearer, protecting these Blackfellas from themselves. But there's so much needs doing for these Blackfellas, the good book straight forward, God helping those that help themselves. More trouble than they're worth & don't want to be helped anyway.

So, this is the last of it, only a dozen Blackfellas left, no land & no more Dreaming, the experiment dead in the water, a waste of resources, Irish & half caste workers with no reason to stay, the buildings abandoned. I see Grandad, leaving for the Western Goldfields & I hear Dad back in Freo, the briefest mention & an inkblot mark on a map. But I know more than I did then, enough now to ask the right questions when I see him.

& I remember Kelvin from the mine, smoke dangling from his mouth & a half smile – Yeah Cuz, mixed blood, but a drop as good as a river I reckon.

***

The last of Don's notes are pushed to the back of the desk, Michael taking a deep breath but has no idea what to think. "It was a long time ago, and even his father was not sure about any of it." Michael stares at the pile of newly read notes, pulls the pressed metal case from his vest pocket and lays it on top of the last pile.

He stands at his desk, yawns and stretches his arms to the ceiling. He wanders past the closed door of the back room to a small sink in Clive's dump of a kitchen. He stares at the stream of cold water, soaps up both hands and scrubs his hands clean, eradicating the smell as best he can. Back at his desk, he brushes the grey curls from his forehead, an eternity since he did any actual `work'. Before ringing Jennifer, Michael runs a finger along the full length of his desk. "Perfectly clean." He turns to Clive's workspace, still piled high with books, papers, pamphlets and a dirty ashtray. He squints. "Ah yes, Clive's French connection."

| 55 |

Don's notes have been liberally dosed with an enzyme cleaner, covered and tucked up tight in plastic, packed in new boxes and are finally gone from the office. Now they sit in a corner of Michael's garage. He expects his old boss to be happy but is not so sure about Jennifer.

Jennifer says Michael has a memory like a steel trap as if it's a good thing. He smiles to himself and stares at the monstera out the office window. "If only I could leave things and just move on, a steel trap no good when I lose half a night's sleep, then dream of Don's packed-up boxes now stuffed in the corner of our garage."

Michael is suddenly aware of his old boss at the desk right behind him, the reflection of Clive's horrid pink cardigan reminding him of a new dalliance between Clive and The Frenchman, both with too much time on their hands. It strikes Michael as ironic, especially considering Clive's secret assessment in the early days; the Frenchman, a teetotal, non-smoker, and Clive always quick to judge: "The Frenchman? A clever man with a dour disposition and a dash too much cologne."

Michael recalls one long liquid lunch at The Prince Hotel

many years ago, an early planning session for Clive's Peru Project, and Clive's insistence on how it would change Michael's life. If only he knew back then how true that would be.

He stares out the window past the tram terminus and the stream of slowed traffic. He is not comfortable with his new glasses and is surprised there has been no mention of his spotlessly clean desk. There are new job files in his desk drawer, but he does not know where to start. And these days, Clive is `big picture' only, with little interest in project details, especially true after the arrival of Don's boxes.

The room is full of smoke like the old days, but this is the new `eager-to-help' Clive. Michael knows his old boss is up to something. He turns and watches Clive puffing on one Gauloises after another, now pouring over his pile of books and papers, his head again in the south of France. He turns in his seat, a brandy in one hand and a cigarette in the other. "I've got to say, Michael, I am damn glad the boxes are finally gone. But I'll tell you something; I'm not prepared to walk away from this, not this time. I'm definitely with The Frenchman on at least checking this out."

"It's just not that far-fetched from where I'm sitting. In fact, I'd class this as a known unknown at worst." He drains his brandy glass. "Anyway, as I said, let's accept his family is from the south. And, let's say his mother's family name goes way back - 'De Alain', was it not?"

Michael nods to himself. "Golly, here we go again." He frowns and has no idea what is coming next. Clive is hunched over his desk and still rummaging among his books, pamphlets, and papers. Michael knows better than to argue once his old boss gets wound up. "So, our best lead is in the south Michael, The Frenchman with time on his hands, back from Quebec and living with Adele in Marseille." Clive turns to Michael. "In the South of France as it happens." Michael knows where Marseille is located and wonders if there is any jealousy there, Clive's old friend Adele and The Frenchman an item after all these years.

Another week passes, with Michael at home. There is a call from The Frenchman himself, and Michael is suspicious, this thing taking on yet another life of its own. "Well, my friend, enough of the small talk. Adele, she takes a train to the Toulouse Library of Studies and Heritage. So, my friend, *oui*, this is about the *Cathari*, The Cathar Heresy, as my old combatant Clive has spoken." Michael sighs, but is listening.

"And I can tell you my friend, in Toulouse where we are looking, the persecution is smaller, more localised. So, we see firsthand what is happening. *Oui*, The Inquisition records, everything, all written down by our good friends, the Catholics. But I will tell you, my friend, Adele's news is not good. It is the 'long shot,' as you say. There is no family name 'De Alain'."

"But Adele, of course, she is stubborn as you know, and follows my own suggestion to travel further afield. Sends me notes. But now we are away from Toulouse, the records not so thorough. And again, there is no family 'Alain.'"

The pause on the other end of the line is forever, and Michael squints. "But, my friend, wait, we do have one name. This name is Joane de Alais."

Michael is still listening. Not the correct name, and yet he feels uncomfortable, the old tingle at the back of his neck. He sits there, aware of the phone line crackling, wondering if he heard The Frenchman right. He is apprehensive of what Clive will say; his old boss is already insistent and bound to be in the office when Michael gets there the following day. The Frenchman is first to break the silence. "And there is more, my friend, something you will want to see when I send it."

In the morning, Michael barely has time to print the French-man's main multi-page attachment when the office front door slams and Clive bursts into the front room. Michael rolls his eyes as his old boss pushes his chair next to Michael, returns with his already overflowing ashtray and makes him-self at home. He snaps up Michael's A4 attachment with a blurred black and white face sheet of Adele and The French-man standing hand in hand. Michael sees no reaction to the picture, his old boss only interested in the content: an intro-ductory paragraph from the Frenchman to Michael, which Clive reads after clearing his throat with a cough.

> "After we spoke last my friend, Adele received a call from an older woman who works for the domestic help section of the Toulouse Municipal Authorities. She says there are so many stories from way back, some related to this Joane de Alais, these stories known by the older community only."

Clive stops, drops the Frenchman's attachment on the desk and stares across at Michael. Michael suspects a trick but has never seen Clive's normally ruddy face so deadly white. Clive coughs again, picks up the attachment and continues.

> "This unfortunate young woman is burned at the stake in 1320, with no cemetery or burial records that Adele can find. I am attaching these town records, however, based on the first dialogue in the local Occitan, translated to the Latin by the Catholic Church. It is Adel's English Translation you see here as the main attachment. We cannot be sure, but *oui*, it must be of interest of course.   *au revoir* / Jean-Paul"

Michael stares across at the attachment on the desk. He had not expected anything new, at best more calculated guesswork. But now he has a load of stories, a crazy dream, an urban myth, and a half-correct name. But still, the tingle is there, up and down the back of his neck. Clive has no such doubts and insists on first sighting the Latin documents on Michael's laptop, a work of art in the flowing hand of some committed Catholic scribe. Although in Latin, Clive is obviously impressed with the strings of names and years.

Both men sit shoulder to shoulder in silence. Clive's attention returns to the attachment, holding the sheets up to the light and closer to his face. Michael pushes Clive's ashtray as far away as possible. Their eyes meet, and Michael accepts there will be no stopping his old boss now.

Clive grabs Michael's arm. "Joane De Alais. Look, I know what you're thinking Michael, but the name could easily have been Anglicized; refugees fleeing north and the English with a big finger in the French pie? Or maybe a later name change, before Don's mother arrived in Australia?" Michael's old boss begins to read Adele's English translation:

> "Testimonies to the Inquisition. Over a number of days. All arrested on the orders of the Bishop on suspicion of Cathar sympathies.
>
> Joane de Alais first appears before the Inquisition on this year of the Lord 1320. After, it came to the attention of the Dominican Inquisitors that Joane de Alais holds the sentiments of the Cathar heresy, especially against the sacrament of the altar.
>
> It is the intention of The Inquisitor to inform himself of the above-mentioned facts and receive the testimonials that follow –
>
> ONE WITNESS: Mother (with five other siblings)
>
> It is now one year past, my heretic husband gone and me left to support six children, the Catholic Church my only protector. On the first occasion I do not recall clearly the season nor the day, but it is my eldest daughter who follows the heresy of my late husband.
> Inquistor asks if Joane went willingly to church?
> Mother answers No Sir, even when reprimanded by the Vicar.
> Inquisitor asks if there were any other sympathies for the heresies of her late husband.
> Mother answers No. Joane was the only wayward child

I implore you sir.

Inquisitor asks the nature of these heresies.

Mother says in the beginning Joane asked how God could be present in the sacrament of the altar. She asked how he could allow himself to be eaten by priests. Joane is already a priestess of their abominable church at seventeen years of age. She is no longer a daughter of mine."

Clive stops every now and then to read ahead, assessing this thing as he goes, one finger keeping his place and picking up where he left off. In the other hand a soggy, half-finished Gauloises is crushed between finger and thumb.

"JOANE DE ALAIS –

The year of the Lord 1320, the Wednesday before the feast of St. James (23 July 1320), there was sent by the Reverend Father in Christ Monsignor Jacques, by the grace of God bishop of Pamiers, a letter of citation against Joane, living in Varilhes, of which the tenor follows: My lord bishop admonished the said Joane that she was guilty of heresy according to information which had been given to him and that she should reply with pure and complete verity on all counts against herself as principal and with others living and dead as witness.

At this admonition and request the said Joane said nothing, neither concerning herself nor concerning others, nor did she wish to do so."

Finally lifting his eyes, Clive turns on his seat and stares directly at Michael. "Well, Michael. Her own mother turned her in. Her own family, for Christ's sake! Can you imagine that? The bastards burned her at the stake while they all stood around and watched!"

Clive drops the attachment back on Michael's desk and pushes it towards Michael. He picks at the sleeve of his pink cardigan and gazes out the office window before turning to Michael. Michael shakes his head. The Frenchman may at least have an open mind, but there is no doubt where Clive stands.

| 56 |

At home, Michael slumps on the living room couch. He has trouble concentrating and admits Clive and The Frenchman make a formidable team. And then there is Jennifer, critical from the beginning of Michael not making a genuine attempt to close out something that clearly bothered him. She worries about this hanging around for another twenty years. Yes, the name may be wrong, and yet it is Michael's reaction that makes her intensely uneasy.

Even Michael knows he must do something, and there is one more loose end that will at least take his mind off this crazier stuff. Michael squints. He already knows the village Don wrote of, often driving through it between Melbourne and home when his father was alive; the very same village a gaggle of houses and a service station. But he took little notice back then, speeding through the old goldfields so often. It was all about the family home and University over forty years ago. He was boarding in Melbourne and always in a hurry.

It seems strange to him now, that he had never thought much of the old Ebenezer Mission or the family home, not until Don and that lodge meeting above Machu Pichu. Those childhood memories had flooded back for whatever reason.

Michael shakes his head. It had been the alcohol talking, but the young writer had obviously taken it all in. And with all he has now read, Michael feels at least partly responsible for Don appearing to change direction in his search for his own answers and leaving his French stories behind.

He has now read all of Don's notes and imagines the house tucked away in the Central Goldfields bush. He had been up and down the highway a hundred times in those University days. And now he feels that country may somehow be part of the bigger puzzle; the almost-myth of the mountain and the village only two hours drive from Melbourne at most.

Michael leaves before Jennifer awakens, with Robbo's mud map and wearing his new glasses. Roadside paddocks flash past, the pastures patchwork, new lambs white, the branches wind-tossed. He glances across at fleeting farmhouses, stands of trees, the post and wire fences from another time. He nods to himself; the glasses are making a difference with the headaches gone. The car radio crackles, a healthy dose of real-world news, the latest Middle East troubles. A drone strike knocks out two Saudi oil refineries.

The village service station looks like it has been closed for years, and Michael leaves the highway. He wonders about the young servo attendant in the baggy hat and passes the old stables and Water Bailiff's cottage. He stops at the irrigation channel, shuts down the engine, and winds down the window. The feeling is strong, like Michael has been out here before, the air heavy with wattle, pungent, and powder yellow, the contact calls of grey currawongs over the sound of water gushing through the sluice gate. He sniffs the village woodsmoke, Don's notes filling his head; the coach road is more of a handful than he expected. Even here, on the edge of the village, deep ruts are full of water. But there is no doubt in his mind, a cluster of plantation pines just here. And there is the ruined tower, right where Robbo's map says it is.

Michael passes the grader wreck pulled off to the side, the machine still there after all these years, no wheels, and the body rusted through. There is another intersection with a lesser track to the south, the tumbled-down stone fences, the broken walls, tailing heaps, and overgrown paths.

He worries about what Jennifer will say when he gets home, the car already filthy. And the track is worse by the minute, the gouges getting deeper, chunks of white quartz dumped on the road from high rock cuttings. He peers down at the map and knows he must be getting close to the goat track, the main track turning west just here, eventually on to the town and the old volcano. But Michael is focused. The car will be fine here; this chicken scratch on Robbo's map shows the route of a three-hour hike. And it suddenly bothers Michael: Did Don just head off this way, the path no longer used and knowing nothing of the house?

Michael is thankful for his daypack being small, locks the car, and imagines the outline of Don's wagon full of building materials; the branches tossed loosely over a rusted bonnet. He kneels down and adjusts the new glasses on his nose; Gracie's old tyre tracks are not obvious but are still there after all these years.

Michael buttons up his vest and jacket, fumbles with the cards in his pocket and stomps across the stony yellow ground. He brushes aside overgrown scrub, stops for a drink of water, and rubs his knee. After three hours, he sees the top of a chimney above the bush, high and skinny, the brick more orange than red. He knows Don's stories, but it still comes as a surprise, more like a picture, a dark-veined creeper in a tangled sprawl at the base of the chimney hearth, the flowers purple. The pungent perfume of the good luck jonquils hangs in the air.

He passes the west wall of the house, the ground steeper up the back. The spur opens out to a majestic stand of white-bowled gums, contrasting with the ubiquitous grey as far as the eye can see. At the edge of the clearing, he tugs at his jacket collar and stands at the base of same toppled giant as Don had. He peers along the length of the trunk and across the blanket of bush to the south. The volcano is not there. He recalls Don's same disappointment when he first arrived, the upturned tree roots throwing a weak spidery shadow. He rubs his fingers on the ancient wood and smells the damp dirt, a row of ants on unknown business along the valleys of moss. Michael raises his head and his eyes drawn south again. There, on the horizon, is the truncated form of the old volcano – 'Grandad's Mount' according to Don – clouds melting to nothing, a splash of sunlight casting a black shadow westward.

Michael imagines the ghosts in the shadow, Don's business, the failed experiment, the church, the self-righteous and patronising of the day, the red brick leftovers, and the desolate cemetery. And then Michael is suddenly back at the beginning, his beginning, the once dormant memories of another place up north called Ebenezer Mission, the Aboriginal kids he still remembers, kicking the footy end to end, those kids punished for speaking their own language. He squints and wonders where they are now.

But Michael is here in the present. He escapes down the hill, a quick circle around the house, the four walls a single room smaller than expected, wallaby droppings on the dirt porch under the veranda. He steps up to the window opening, startled by the chirp of a swallow that buzzes his ear. Michael shakes his head. What are another twenty years in the overall scheme of things?

A stiff push of the door reveals the timber floor, one patch of boards newer than the others, each step hollow. He leans back, instinctively pulls the door closed behind him, squints in the gloom, and waits for his eyes to adjust. The inside is dusty, and he coughs. Michael turns to the window and peers outside to the gully down the hill. He waves his hand in front of his face catching cobwebs on his fingers. A long-handled broom stands by the door but tumbles to the floor with a loud bang.

He feels guilty again, the same as when reading Don's notes, the cards in his vest pocket not helping. Being here makes the whole thing even more personal if that was possible. There are scrapes in the dust on the floor; something dragged. Michael imagines Don moving his latest box to the door, more notes for safekeeping at Robbo's, or maybe Robbo himself, collecting his friend's belongings and ducking his head to get out the door. Michael scratches the side of his head, wondering if Robbo had planned for the boxes to sit in his garage for over twenty years while he tried to forget that final night and the freakish death of his best friend.

Michael peers around, doubting there would have been

much in the way of furnishings, not with Don always travelling light: maybe some dried food, Michael's borrowed books and his, the busted satchel loaded with his latest notes. Michael stares at the far corner, a bare bunk pushed against the wall, Spartan style, the wood rough and unfinished, a tired-looking mat, a khaki sleeping bag, and a table in the opposite corner near the hearth. The table is small, like something from a discarded tea party setting with wooden slats and skinny legs. A black plastic fruit crate sits alongside.

Another currawong calls from the bush outside. Michael wanders over to the crate, sits, and slumps forward. He takes a deep breath, runs his hand along the table edge, and blows the dust off his finger. Something catches his eye on the floor through a gap in the table. He squints, preferring not to disturb a thing, sits bolt upright, and prods his new glasses on the bridge of his nose, the disconcerting tingle on the back of his neck. A card lay covered in dust.

He reaches down and fumbles, the lone card badly bent with three corners missing. He holds it closer, the feeble light just enough. He blows off the top layer of dust and wipes the card with his paisley shirt sleeve, the back floral and familiar. His other hand gravitates to his vest and fiddles with the case in his pocket.

Michael flips the card over. That mystery is solved at least, the missing card here all the time, from before Don's death, the identical flowery, diamond-cobbled back, the ancient washed-out browns and reds. His fingers tremble, and he stands, holding the card to the light from the window opening. He squints, rotates the picture, and stares at a man hanging upside down. He is dressed in Medieval garb with red leggings and a blue waistcoat with the chest embroidered. Michael feels odd, hypnotized by the figure so rigid and controlled. He shakes his head. One leg is straight, the other bent. It strikes Michael that the man is suspended by a spider web and anchored by the moon, a tilted waxing crescent afloat a black and starry sky. Both the man's arms are bent, hands behind his back. The messy red hair is somehow contradictory. Michael peers closer. A half mask hides the eyes and face.

Suddenly aware of his tight grip, he twists the card between his finger and thumb. His thoughts are a million miles away: chatting with Don's best friend in Fremantle over twenty years ago, Robbo the beanpole in a flannelette shirt and jeans. Then suddenly, back in Melbourne, Robbo again, living with his family and working offshore, Michael with a new job, ambitious, his life split between home and the office. Both had moved on from the funeral, or tried to, even though Clive had grilled Michael for weeks afterwards. Robbo's wife Anne had insisted her husband collect whatever was left at the old house: Don's last box of notes, the books, and other bits and pieces.

The card is still in Michael's hand, and he hesitates. Clive is right about the whole thing refusing to go away. "So, this really is the missing card from the pack gifted to Don by his mother on his sixteenth birthday and lying here under the table, at least since 1997."

| 57 |

Michael sits at his study desk, Robbo on the other end of the phone. "Yep, Mike, the least I can do... to see how you're getting on with D's stuff. Feeling a bit guilty, I s'pose, dumpin' them boxes in your lap like that. Have to admit, I did try and forget them until Anne and me were downsizing, that is. Then I couldn't put it off any longer, not with Anne on the case. She's been trying to get me to sort those bloody boxes for years. To be honest, Mike, I guess I just didn't wanna know."

"Anyway, you goin' up to the house got me thinkin', needing to touch base and say thanks. You know... Maricielo really was D's best chance to get himself sorted, I reckon. We still chat, calling her now and then. But she never wanted those boxes. Too close to the bone, I reckon. Same with his dad. And I'm no bloody reader, never have been."

Michael senses Robbo is also uncomfortable after all these years but wonders why Angela did not take Don's boxes. She was his sister after all. "Yep Mike, she would have taken them for sure, but..."

"Angie? Mmmm, shit... you didn't know? So sorry Mike,

my bad… been gone for years… died not long after Don as it happens… that family cursed or something."

Michael stops breathing, then gasps. Now it was his turn to feel guilty for making no effort to stay in touch with Robbo and Maricielo after the funeral. Just too keen to drop the whole thing. And he feels terrible about putting poor Robbo on the spot after all this time, having to relive something like that.

"Relive it? Oh… well, I do owe you, Mike… takin' those bloody boxes no small thing. Mmmm… long time ago now, you and me back in Melbourne after the funeral… Angie in the US. Angie & me? Well… we could always talk. Even sent me a five-page thank you note after the funeral."

"Seemed all rosy at first… the wedding, I mean… all goin' well, and Jackson OK. They were comfortable in Los Angeles, with everything she needed, and the locals friendly. A bit worried though, about how Jackson would cope with her and five cats all up."

Michael recalls Angela from the funeral, the understandable shock of her brother's death, the drinking and pills, and her trying hard to keep it together. But now he has read Don's notes, Angela was always a powerful presence.

"So… I'd read Angie's five-page note Mike, somethin' not right. I rang her that night… the accident and funeral still pretty raw. Then it was like a dam broke or somethin'… her blurting the whole thing out. She'd lost patience with Jackson's black magic bullshit and resented the money he gave to some faceless guru she'd never met. She said the bad days outnumbered the good, bloody peeved that she'd given up a good career."

"And get this, Mike, as if she didn't have enough on her plate with D's accident and moving to The States: there'd been trouble... it's all coming back to me... local burglaries and stuff, she said. Yep... not good... her ringin' the police more than once. She was bloody angry with LA's finest ignoring her, somethin' Angie was not used to. They were always busy and not interested, she said. No resources to investigate every call from a paranoid Aussie woman scared of her own shadow."

Michael can easily imagine how she took that: not well. He can see her fuming, sucking on her Benson and Hedges; hear the rattle and clunk of her bracelet. He can imagine poor Robbo holding the phone, saying little, and still sorting the funeral fallout in his own head, like Michael; Robbo just back from cleaning out Don's house up the bush back then.

"Yep... you bet... I remember it, Mike, felt pretty bad, I have to say. It seems Angie sat around to all hours, alone and in the dark, no TV, no radio. She missed D real bad, his silly stories whirling around her head, lots of booze, and just staring out the window. Yep, she'd love to have his bloody boxes." Robbo goes quiet, needing time to pull his own memories together.

"Well... I can tell you, she wasn't happy with Jackson at all... not right on top of the accident... never home apparently, work meetings with his gurus. Or maybe another woman. She never knew."

"Looking back at the funeral, I think she changed... we all changed. And by the time I called, she'd absolutely come to her senses about that marriage. Said it was the dumbest thing she'd ever done. D had never commented on Jackson, but yep, always a funny choice in my book."

"To be honest, Mike, she went on a bit, seemed determined to set the record straight with anyone that would listen, thought she could twist Jackson around her little finger at first... change him somehow. She had lived with D's stories all her life, no intention of falling for Jackson's sleight-of-hand Eastern religious stuff."

"And look... there was something else... something she'd never told us. Just too crazy, she said, D ringing her the night before he was killed. D couldn't sleep, apparently. It was early in LA, and Angie in the middle of wedding stuff. She promised to ring him back, but that never happened. So... Angie's got another serious dose of the guilts right there. Join the club I reckon."

"And this is where it gets real bloody murky, her losing the plot I reckon. She'd had some sort of dream herself, just before I rang... insists I hear about it: a stressed kid... sick-looking, barely a teenager, and comin' out of nowhere in the middle of the night. Angie said the face was too white, said it was unreal, a long blue dress and a shit load of smoke, the floor all wet and a rotten smell."

Michael feels sick, the now familiar electric tingle on the back of his neck. Robbo's voice startles him.

"Still there Mike? Look, I know it was just a dream... I get that. But really, she was so shook up about it... You should have heard her voice. I'm thinking D's death has put a cracker under her, yep, somethin' she carried with her after the funeral.

But then, the phone went dead or somethin'... thought I'd

lost her. I mean, like… is she still there? Is that broken glass I heard? Hope she's OK."

"Anyway, Angie's back on the line, whispering about that damn dream, like the girl in blue is right there at the window," Robbo's voice stops mid-sentence, "a sick kid like she's in the middle of chemo something, reaching out and no hair."

Robbo coughs. "So… next day Maricielo gets a call in Freo. She's dead, Mike, bloody dead… just like that. A Meth Lab down the road, some crazy nutter after cash, a break-in, and the bloke way off his head. Nasty stuff, apparently." Robbo hangs up, leaving Michael feeling dizzy. He leaves the study but tells Jennifer nothing of Robbo's call.

Michael drives to work as if nothing has happened and pulls over at the café mid-morning. A million thoughts fill his head, and he sits on a bentwood chair at a round table outside and on its own. He stares at the passing stream of traffic but sees nothing, oblivious to the clamour of trams as they come and go at the nearby terminus. He still has Don's cards in his vest pocket.

He turns to see Maria, her head above the top of her coffee machine, the familiar bob with a streak of white. Michael squints. Maria. She knows some of the story: Don leaving Michael the cards in 1997, and Michael trying to forget the accident until Don's boxes arrived this year.

Maria appears at Michael's shoulder, those big glasses with the scarlet frames. She frowns. "Sooo Lover, we don't see you so much these days. And what do you have for us? You have so neglected your Maria, and I am expecting something special." Her hands are on her hips, but they drop to her sides when Michael does not answer. Instead, he pulls the cards from his corduroy vest pocket and lay the embossed metal case flat on the table. His index finger settles on the lid, the fine cheque pattern and then the simple cross in the centre.

Maria fakes disappointment, pouts then leans closer. "Ah *si*, it is about the cards, of course, but Lover, you are always so sweet to your Maria in the past, and yet now I am old, you forget me. But Clive, he drops by to see your Maria, tells me you have found the missing card. You keep this secret from poor Maria?"

Michael's face is pale with a weak smile. He has nowhere to run. Don's mother, Don, and Angela are all dead and he finally opens the case, setting the lid gently aside. The top card has three corners missing and is browner than the others. Maria leans closer, lifts it from the box and studies it carefully. She nods her head. "Finally, Lover. So, this is the missing upside-down man, *si, Il Traditore.* The Traitor, he finally comes home."

Maria rises to her full height, pouts her lips, and waves a finger in Michael's face. "Not like you, Lover, always so sure of yourself. This card is deep water, everything not as it seems."

REFERENCES

All text Copyright © Ian Cochrane 2023
National Library of Australia Cataloguing-in-Publication data:
    Cochrane, Ian James, 1951
Cards and Clay – one man two worlds /
    Ian Cochrane, 1st edition p-book, 1st edition e-book
Subjects:
Cochrane, Ian James, 1951
Fiction
Historical fiction
Mystery
Travel
Tarot
Religion
Australia
Australian Aboriginal
France
Cathars
South America
Peru
Incas